Demonologist Luke Melloy has seen the face of pure evil. He's fought it and sent it back to hell. It's what he does. To Claire Westin, ghosts and demons are just great television and good for ratings. When she's faced with the truth Luke has seen, her reality is turned upside down as the two are swept into dire straits moments after they meet. Desire sparks between the unlikely pair, throwing their hearts into chaos with a love neither of them expected nor wanted.

When the Demon targets an unsuspecting Claire with his wrath, Luke finds his focus split between his oath to God and the awakening of his heart. Together, can they face the ancient evil and defeat it, or will they lose everything?

Finders
Copyright © 2019 Amy Romine
ISBN: 978-1-4874-2596-8
Cover art by Martine Jardin

Published by eXtasy Books Inc or
Devine Destinies, an imprint of eXtasy Books Inc

Look for us online at:
www.eXtasybooks.com or www.devinedestinies.com

FINDERS
FINDERS GHOST HUNTING BOOK 1

BY

AMY ROMINE

DEDICATION

This book is dedicated to Ed and Lorraine Warren for their tireless battle against the forces of evil in this world.

To Jason Hawes and Grant Wilson, the founders of Ghost Hunters as well as the entire Ghost Hunters Team from which this book was inspired.

I would also like to thank all of the ghost hunters that helped in research and development of this book, specifically Chris King and the Oklahoma Paranormal Research group as well as ghost hunting investigators Paul Stevenson, Jasmine Clark, Cody and Miranda Glenn, Renee Hicks, Diandra Rogers, William Brown, and John.

Lastly, to my loving and supportive family and friends whose endless patience and feedback made this book possible.

CHAPTER ONE

Two Years Ago

The hot sun beat down on television producer Claire Westin's bare shoulders. A cloudless sky and a soft breeze accompanied her on a walk through the fields behind her house in Claremore, Oklahoma.

Her dog, Pip, ran free in and out of the brush chasing crickets and barking at turtles. This was her place of solace and calm. With her cell phone turned off, she let go of the hectic rhythm of her life, basking in the music of nature. She followed the neatly mowed path, knowing the steps by heart, walking along with her mind blank and calm. Suddenly the music stopped. Silence. Hearing the rattle of a snake, she turned to her left and called out to her dog.

"Pippy?"

Something shadowed the sun. Her eyes traveled over the empty field to the source of the shadow. A hooded figure stood tall against the light of the sun. Her body froze in place. Then the air evaporated, followed by blackness

Present Day

Professor of Demonic Theory Luke Melloy's melodic calm voice guided the theater full of attentive theology students through an expanse of images projected on the far wall.

"From the devil reigning over the souls of the damned, to the famed self-portrait from the Codex Gigas, the trickery, the promises, the feelings of desire, and euphoria are all methods of seduction. A Demon's goal is to make you believe something is missing and they have whatever you need to fill the gap in your life. Salvation, more time, love, money, power — whatever your deepest desire, the Demon will discover it and use it against you. It's a carrot on a string, pulling you further and further down the path until there is no way back.

"Now, if you think this is all some blatant flirtation, it's not. The seduction or infestation is very subtle. This persuasion, for lack of a better term, takes place in your subconscious, feeding you the lies and the promises in the white noise you are not consciously hearing."

Luke's students — most of them — clung to every word. As a tenured Professor of Demonology, he taught a specialized class at the Catholic Seminaries across the country. This semester he found himself in Lander, WY. He personally chose his students based on rigorous testing and one-on-one interviews. To delve into the depths of theological lore of a very dark nature, his students had to be of a particular mindset to attend his class.

"There's a famous quote by a scholar of sorts. *The biggest trick the devil ever pulled was convincing the world he doesn't exist.* There's truth in the statement. Millions don't believe in hell, demons, or the devil. Even more, believe in nothing at all. Tell me, who is the easiest to sway? A person with faith–whether it be faith in a Higher Power or faith in each other or basic humanity–or a person who has no faith in anything at all?"

A bell rang, and the lights turned on. "Think about it. The assignment is fifteen-hundred words by Tuesday. Enjoy the day."

As he packed up his desk, a familiar face appeared from the crowd, approaching the front of the auditorium. Luke extended his hand to his longtime friend, Grant Henley. "Grant, I was just packing up to go meet you."

Standing six-foot-five, with broad shoulders, a shaved head and a neatly trimmed goatee, Grant Henley, when judged on looks alone, was intimidating. Luke knew better, having worked with Grant intermittently over the years. He'd never met a more empathetic, generous, and kind man in his life. When Grant and *Finders*, his ghost hunting team, came across a case of the demonic plaguing innocents, he called Luke, a professionally experienced demonologist, to intervene.

"I admit I left a little early to catch your lecture. Enthralling, as always."

"Enthralling is a little much, but I try to keep my students' attention."

"How many of them know about your firsthand experience with these afflictions?"

"All of them. I'm upfront and honest about all of my dealings. I use case files as examples. It's the only way to make them aware of the reality. Theory and lore can only go so far."

"How does the Council feel about your transparency?"

Luke knew how Grant had, on many occasions, been forced to experience the bureaucracy of the Catholic Council firsthand when it came to assisting innocents being tortured by demonic entities. It was not easy to persuade them of anything.

Luke laughed, shoving his computer in his bag. "My teaching techniques are an ongoing debate."

"You never wanted it easy."

"Yeah, right," Luke glanced down at the only remaining item on his desk. Unconsciously flinching at the headline, he tapped his fingers. Luke's mind flashed to the sight of his friend and colleague hanging from the steeple of the Seminary.

"Sorry about Father Daniel. I saw the paper when I was getting coffee," Grant said. "Did you two work together?"

"On occasion," Luke said, tossing the paper in the recycle bin.

"The media presence out front is because of what happened?" Grant asked.

"The Council refuses to give the press any details. Thus, the media are looking for any stray information they can get."

"Good thing I parked out back."

"Not a bad idea." Luke slung his bag over his shoulder. "What's the latest with *Finders?*"

"Besides you as the newest member of the team?"

"I'm still undecided. This little excursion is a trial run."

"Understood. Have you been watching the show?"

"When I have the time. I'll admit I'm a little behind, but I assume it's not much different from when there are no cameras. Just fewer people and lighting."

"You got it."

Reality television producer Claire Westin took a long gulp of her coffee, knowing to answer the telephone call had been a mistake. Executive Producer Walt Hemmings' latest rant would last at least another thirty to forty-five seconds.

"Again, I need you back here at six for the strategy meetings, and we are gonna need interviews from each of the writers and the entourage teams."

Claire swallowed the last of the coffee before responding, "Walt, we had this discussion on Friday. I'm in Wyoming working on the Crestwater case with *Finders*. I won't be back until at least Saturday at the earliest."

"Where are you again?"

"Crestwater, Wyoming," Claire repeated.

"What a fucking mess," Walt cursed.

Claire rolled her eyes, tired of having this same conversation with him. Despite the fact Walt was not the showrunner for the ghost hunting reality show, he insisted on micromanaging her decisions. Walt Hemmings had successfully launched three franchises and was in the midst of his fourth in a matter of five years. His latest endeavor, *The Cocktail Party,* for which Claire worked as a producer, was a scavenger-hunt challenge-driven reality show allowing undiscovered writers to have high-powered agents hear their pitches. An unprecedented opportunity for unknown authors to have their ideas green-lighted, if they met and conquered the challenges. The show included lots of drama, creative collaboration — aka more drama — and the thrill of the hunt.

"It's fine."

"Allowing the show's co-anchor to simply exit is not fine."

"Contractually, I had no grounds to force him to stay," Claire replied, then muttered under her breath. "I wouldn't have forced him to if I had."

"Bullshit, Claire, the standard — "

"Walt, the *Finders* contract with Westin Media is independent. Grant and Jason have full creative and editing control. We provide the infrastructure to support production. It's a sixty-forty split. Therefore, I have no control or grounds to dictate who works on the show or for how long."

"Who the hell approved the contract?"

"I did," Claire said with a broad smile and a sense of satisfaction. *Finders* was her baby from the beginning. She'd brought the show to her father's attention, then done the negotiating, the contracting, and the producing. If she was going to be a part of the Westin Media empire, it was going to be on her terms.

"I'll be back by Saturday, hopefully. Thanks, Walt."

Despite Walt trying to get a few final words in, Claire disconnected the blue tooth, ending the call.

"I think the conversation went well. What do you think, Pip?" Claire asked the mid-sized Catahoula-boxer mix lying in the passenger seat.

Her faithful companion and best friend barked in response.

She gave his scruff a scratch. He sat up, looking out the front window. The GPS directed her to make a right. Pip growled. The GPS disconnected. Claire pulled over to reset the phone, while Pip stood on the seat, looking tense.

"Now look at what you've done. You broke it."

The dog whimpered in response.

"Just kidding. Calm down. I know we're far from home, but it's fresh air and gorgeous here. Lighten up, will you?" The phone reset, and still no GPS signal. "Looks like we're going to have to find this place the old-fashioned way."

Claire brought up a picture of the church on her phone before attaching the phone to the hands-free cradle. She followed the steep narrow tree-lined road, searching for any signs or indications of houses, buildings, or churches. Mailboxes or well-marked driveways seemed to be non-existent. She drove a few more miles and was about to give up until Pip barked, bringing her attention to a small opening in the tree line. Claire slowed, debated, and went for it, making the tight right turn. The small opening widened. She drove through. A few miles later, the familiar caravan of four black SUVs and a large black van with the *Finders* logo plastered on the side brought a smile to her face.

Craig, the *Finders'* tech producer, appeared from the corner of the van waving. Claire pulled up next to him and parked her truck. A bitter wind cut at her neck as she exited the vehicle. She pulled the collar of her coat up against the barrage.

"You found it. We were getting worried."

"No thanks to the GPS," Claire replied, opening the passenger door and letting Pip out. He immediately ran to Craig, greeting him warmly before running off into the woods, she assumed to relieve himself. Speaking of which, she could use a bathroom break.

Finders consisted of a team of eight to ten paranormal investigators. The supporting technical team was four boom operators and four cameramen. Depending on the size of the other locations, they could have more or fewer. For the investigation of Crestwater Church, Craig and Claire had doubled the number of cameras to enable multiple teams to be filming concurrently. In addition to the film equipment, the paranormal team employed a slew of scientific equipment to collect evidence of paranormal activity during the investigation. With the entire team at work, it would take a full day to set up and calibrate all of the necessary equipment.

The flurry of activity continued around her. Team members waved and said hello. Claire nodded, smiling in response. "How are we looking?" she asked Craig.

"Four hours until sundown, six until lights out. We're right on schedule. I was just about to go around to the back of the church for some B-Roll shots. The foliage is amazing, and the shots I'm getting are phenomenal."

"Is the church open?"

"Yeah, we haven't locked it down for dinner yet."

"Cool, the three Venti Starbucks on the trip here are calling for an exit."

"Gotcha," Craig replied with a smile and a nod.

Claire inhaled the fresh air. Despite the cold, it was invigorating. She drank up the smell of wood, freshly fallen leaves, and dirt. Taking a closer look at the church, she realized the media photos didn't do justice to the immense structure.

Dark redwood covered the fifty-foot face. Jutting into the sky like a dagger, the roof was pointed and peaked ten feet above the face. The aged wood's hues shifted with the sunlight, and the sway of trees gave the appearance of the inanimate object breathing. Against the backdrop of the autumn leaves, the sight was staggering and breathtaking. Claire ventured to the wide-mouth doorway opening of the church.

Piles of orange and yellow cords looked like snakes spilling out the open windows. The crunching of leaves beneath her feet and the whipping of the wind made her stride a little quicker. Hurrying up the plethora of steps, she lifted the red *hot set* tape barrier out of the way and pushed open the door.

As she stepped into the vestibule, the stale air stifled her lungs. The solid wooden door closed behind her, but sunlight continued to stream into the enclosed area via the large windows on either side. Thick darkness beyond the sun's reach constricted the expanse. Even the doors were massive, at twice her height, at least. She guessed they were made from solid walnut, from the ancient trees surrounding the church.

A chilling wisp crept within her hair to the back of her neck, like fingers playing with her hair. Claire instinctively turned. Seeing nothing but feeling a shiver up her spine, she took in the surroundings and searched for the bathroom. Eying a promising door, she made a beeline and found salvation.

Thankfully the facilities were in working order. After washing her hands in cold water, Claire dried them on her jeans. Taking a quick look in the cracked mirror, she adjusted her long brown hair tied up in a ponytail, smoothing any unruly strands and bumps before walking back into the vestibule.

The intricately carved stone lining the archway into the nave caught her eye, and she stopped, inspecting it closer. A carved frame of tree limbs with gnarled and knotted extensions bent and twisted around the mouth of the doorway, amazingly delicate and detailed. She could feel the bark beneath her fingertips despite knowing it was carved in stone.

Hearing Pip barking at the door, Claire moved away from the nave archway to the main entrance. Opening it, she saw no sign of her dog. Confused, she walked outside to the steps.

"Pip? Pippy, come!"

The flurry of activity when she'd arrived had ceased. The *Finders* crew had disappeared, and Claire remembered Craig mentioning dinner. Hearing another bark, she followed the sound.

"Pippy, come!" Claire said, her patience waning. She wasn't used to Pip not obeying her commands. They were going to need to talk. Finally, the dog appeared, sprinting out of the thick brush. She breathed an unconscious sigh of relief.

"Claire?"

Her heart leaped as Pip barked.

She spun toward the voice, seeing nothing but Pip taking off through the open door of the church. "Pippy!"

Claire chased after him, into the vestibule, but saw no sign of him. He barked again. The sound was muffled. He had to be on the other side of the large arched doors leading to the nave. Claire pulled on the slightly open door. It swept back with a whoosh of air and a loud thud, the sound echoing off the brittle walls, and a shower of dust rained down.

"Fuck. Pip, come here!" she yelled, attempting to not choke within the cloud of decay from the ruin.

Seriously?

Claire grabbed her phone, turning on the flashlight feature, utilizing it to explore. She shivered at the feel of invisible hands pulling her deeper into the darkness. Heart thudding and hands shaking, she struggled to remain calm, though her mind told her to run.

High cathedral ceilings jutted up to the heavens. Faded images of angels and cherubs adorned the beams. The pews remained, dust-covered and overrun by spiders. When the light flashed over the stone altar at the head of the room, Claire's heart skipped.

The sound of metal clanked on the floor, and Claire panicked, thinking she'd dropped her keys. Checking her pocket, she found her keys intact. Using her flashlight, she searched the surrounding floor for the source of the noise. Her eyes focused on a large old-fashioned key a few inches from where she stood. Reaching down, she picked it up. The cold metal felt icy in her hand. She examined it closely.

Pip barked. Claire turned, putting the key in her pocket, and realized how far away from the opening she'd traveled. Pip's fur brushed against her legs. She turned, glaring at him. "You and I are going to talk about this."

"Claire!"

She heard her name and turned. A scorched skull atop a body shrouded in black dominated her vision. Claire instinctively raised her arms, stepping back. The floor beneath her cracked before disappearing from beneath her feet. Her body fell. She screamed. The light above quickly faded, and wet darkness engulfed her senses. The impact rendered her immobile while agonizing pain from icy water shocked her entire body.

With her arms flailing, her senses returned. She struggled to kick her legs despite the hardening of her muscles. *Up, I need to go up!*

Pushing her arms in front of her, willing the blackness away, she prayed for air.

CHAPTER TWO

A cold crisp wind swirled around the black SUV as it followed its highway path on their way to Crestwater, Wyoming, making Luke shudder.

"*Finders* doesn't work much differently from the way you do," Grant explained, driving through the winding roads as Luke listened. "People call us, or on occasion, we come across locations experiencing an unnatural disturbance. With a description of the events, we talk to the residents and research the history of the property. Due to the show's popularity, we screen carefully against lots of hacks and wannabes looking for attention. If the information checks out, we schedule a visit. We try to schedule several things in the same area at the same time. Like this trip, we have the church, a residence, and a library on the schedule."

Taking in Grant's words, Luke shifted his broad shoulders, adjusting to the confines of the seat. "Explain the process. Do you record everything for the show, or just some?"

"We record everything, then decide what's worthy and what's not. Sometimes it's not up to us. There are occasions where the families don't want their experiences televised. They don't want the exposure. The cases become very personal. As you know, I started this team first and foremost to help those in need. The details of the investigation and whether it makes it through the network's cutting room are secondary."

"Glad to hear the media monster hasn't completely corrupted your brain." Luke shifted his focus to the windshield while his haunted past of personal paranormal nightmares mixed with the bitter cold.

Grant and his team had gained notoriety and financial gain for their ghost hunting, but from all accounts, none of the fame had gone to their heads. The purpose of *Finders* was steadfast — the education and assistance of those in need.

"What's on the menu?"

"Clare, our producer, stumbled on this one. Crestwater Church." Grant went over the details. "There is some question as to whether the girl was traumatized by events at the church or by something her boyfriend may have done to her at the church. We're looking to at least shed some light on the paranormal aspect."

"Sounds like a lot of pressure," Luke recalled seeing bits of the story on the local news.

"Yep, and exposure. Here we are."

Grant turned off the highway onto a narrow dirt road. The large church came into view. Luke had expected a Gothic marvel but instead was faced with curved lines and a sleek exterior. Surrounded by trees, the accompanying cemetery was overgrown and thick with vegetation. Grant stopped the SUV behind another identical vehicle.

The pair exited the truck, taking in the surroundings. They both hesitated at the sound of a barking dog. "Do you hear that?"

"Sounds like a dog. Do the owners have a dog?" Luke asked.

"No, but our producer Claire does. Wonder what's—" Grant stopped at the sight of Craig charging toward the truck.

Submerged in icy water, Claire's body screamed in protest. Her sensibility kicked in, pushing away the panic. She consciously released some air out of her lungs. Following the bubbles, she swam toward the surface. Breaking the crest of water, she gulped in the air despite its stinging in her chest. Coughing the water out, Claire tried to take in her surroundings.

Where the hell am I?

Reaching out her arms, she estimated the diameter of the area was about eight feet. Water and, from the feel of the cold texture beneath her fingertips, stone walls. A well? She'd fallen into a well? Wait, no, she didn't fall. The memory of the horrific face before the cold and blackness caused her heart to race. Claire shoved herself against the wall, searching the darkness and listening intently for any movement in the water. Any sign of her attacker. Quiet. Silent.

She looked upward for sunlight. It was there, but it seemed very far away.

"Help! Craig, Help!" Claire called upward, her voice weak and cracking. Hearing Pip's barking gave her some small reassurance Craig would find her sooner rather than later. "Pip, go get Craig! Pippy, go find Craig!"

She heard another few barks and then silence. She was alone in the dark well, and her imagination crept in on her consciousness. Her clothes were heavy in the cold water. Claire clung to the stone wall, hooking her feet and fingers into the cracks to keep herself above the surface. Deciding to focus on a way out in case help was taking too long, she felt for handholds leading her up and out of the well.

Something brushed against her leg. Claire hesitated and refocused on the task at hand.

It's only whatever plant life has sprung up down here. Hell, it could be a freaking fish, for all I know.

The occurrence repeated. Claire recoiled, listening for any sign of mischief.

Nothing.

Claire took a deep breath, forcing her heart to calm.

It is a big bowl of water. There's nothing down here but you,

Claire.

"Claire?"

"Craig! Craig, I'm here!" Claire yelled, the sound of his voice giving her an instant surge of adrenaline. "Get me out of here! Please!"

"Grant! Help me get the lines out of the truck!" Luke heard Craig shout.

"What's happened?" Grant said.

"Claire fell into a well."

"What?" Grant followed Craig to the back of the adjacent SUV, Luke behind him.

They opened the rear doors, revealing stacks of equipment. Craig and Grant immediately grabbed rolls of two-hundred-feet extension cables. Grant handed one to Luke, then took one himself.

"Follow me." Craig turned in a run. The dog waited for them before leading the three men to the well, a gaping hole in the floor. "Claire! I got the lines. Hang on!" Craig yelled.

A small, weak voice echoed from the darkness, along with a sloshing sound. "Hurry."

"Is that water?" Grant asked.

"It's a well," Craig said.

"We need to hurry," Luke said. The men uncoiled the cabling and secured the lines together. Luke peered down into the hole, seeing only black. "Do you have a flashlight?"

"In the truck, beneath the front seat," Grant replied.

Luke nodded. As he ran back to the truck, his mind spun with other things they may need while he was there. A blanket would be helpful. He spotted a moving pad thrown over the equipment. Grabbing hold of the corner, he pulled, and it fell out. Next he opened the passenger door, ducked, and found a heavy, large, black flashlight under the seat. *Perfect.* Wasting no time, he rejoined Craig and Grant who were ready to lower the makeshift rope into the well.

"Wait!" They stopped. Luke tied the flashlight to the end of the cabling, giving them an anchor and Claire some light. "Okay, go."

"It's coming down, Claire. There's a flashlight on the end. When you get it, turn it on," Grant called into the well.

Pip barked at him as if relaying the words.

A bitter wind slapped at the group, reminding them of the dropping temperatures.

"Craig, go start the truck, turn the heat up full blast." Craig nodded and disappeared. "Claire, can you see it?" The men looked at each other when there was no answer, "Claire, can you hear me?"

"Yes, I've got it."

A light at the bottom of the well turned on. The group could barely see Claire in the beam.

"Do you think you can climb out?" Grant asked.

"I-I think I can," she replied.

"Grant, she may be too cold," Luke said, thinking of the freezing water and the chance of hypothermia setting in.

"What other option do we have?"

"I can climb down the line and bring her up."

Grant contemplated the scenario. "Let's try this first."

The dog placed his front paws on the edge of the well peering down.

"What's happening?" Craig asked, rejoining the men at the edge of the well.

"Claire is trying to climb out," Grant said.

There was no light except for the swinging flashlight at the bottom of the well. Luke could see it moving as Claire attempted to scale the side of the well.

Grant called, "How are you doing, Claire?"

"So far, so good. I'm going to need Starbucks after this. Just warning you."

Grant smiled along with Craig. "You can have anything you want."

Rough stones piled on top of one another created a patchwork of brown-gray hues. Smooth to the touch, the rocks were affected by hundreds of years of water wear.

"Damn right I'm getting whatever I want," Claire said aloud, trying in vain to dry her hands, cursing the extra ten pounds from her water-logged clothes. "A hot Venti Toffee-Nut-Latte, double shot." She started her climb, grasping the cold, slick plastic cord in her hands. "A scalding shower with warm, soft terry cloth towels, heated slippers, and another hot coffee."

Claire briefly thanked her trainer, Jorge, for making her develop her upper body strength. Using the cord along with jutting rock footholds, Claire started up the well. Ignoring the swinging flashlight's creation of odd shapes and reflections off the water, she focused upward on the light and sound from above.

The trek was slow going, but she seemed to be halfway there, judging from the size of the opening at the top.

Hot shower, hot coffee, you can do this.

Looking up, she saw something falling toward her in the darkness. Hugging the wall, she yelped when it hit. Something grabbed her shoulders, throwing her back. Her head hit the wall hard. She never knew what people meant by seeing stars until then. Losing her grip, she plummeted back down into the cold water. The shock of the icy water hit again. She kicked to return to the surface. Feeling something wrap around her ankle, she focused on her feet and saw a skull-like face. Her adrenaline soaring, she kicked and struggled to free her ankle. She managed to break free, breaching the surface, gasping for air.

A few more moments of deafening silence passed. Luke looked at Grant. Pip growled at the darkness, showing his teeth. The sound of shifting stone followed by a scream got their attention.

"Claire, are you okay?" Grant called.

The sound of a splash echoed off the stone walls. The flashlight swung freely, the light dancing off the water.

Luke searched the darkness of the well. "Claire?"

The water broke to the sound of gasping and struggling.

Grant and Craig called out to her again, while Pip barked wildly.

"Grant, Craig, anchor me," Luke told them.

Both men grabbed hold of the cabling, as did Luke, the coating slick and cold in his hands. Below them, more splashing and gasping. Luke leaned into the well, using his feet against the well wall for stabilization. Walking his way down, he kept his hands tight around the cord. A lack of sound from the bottom of the well spurred his movements.

"Claire?" he called.

He heard her gasp again. Her head broke through the water. She seemed to be struggling to stay afloat. "Hang on, Claire. I'm almost there."

The water broke again. Silence.

"Claire?"

When he got no response, Luke released his hold, letting his body fall. The frigid water enveloped him quickly, his muscles screaming from the shock. The water seemed to be deep, his feet not touching the bottom. Grasping the flashlight, he struggled to untie it, confusion and worry searing his brain.

There's not much room down here. Where is she?

Not seeing any sign of Claire, he took a breath, submerging himself. Using the flashlight, he searched the water. Shocked to see the depth of the well, he found her several feet below him, long brown hair billowing around her struggling face. Luke swam to her, wrapping his arm around her waist to pull her up.

Claire shook her head, pointing down. Luke saw something wrapped around her leg. Luke adjusted, tugging and pulling on what seemed to be a weed until it released its hold. Cresting the water, he gasped for air, seeing her emerge.

"You okay?" Luke asked, holding her tight against him. From the coldness of her body, he knew the answer. She nodded weakly.

"Claire, Luke, can you hear us?" Grant called, and Pip barked.

"Yeah, we're here," Luke called back, looking to Claire. "You think you can hang on to me?" Shivering and teeth chattering, she nodded, her bright blue eyes focused and alert. "Okay, let's get out of here."

Luke started his climb up, commanding his muscles to stay engaged. Only a few more feet and they would be out. A loud rumble followed by the screeching of metal got his attention.

"Water!"

Claire's voice focused his mind. The water was rising exponentially. Luke quickened his pace. Metal. Luke stopped dead, seeing a flurry of activity above them. A metal grate had positioned itself at the top of the well, trapping them. Water rising, no way out. They were in trouble. "Grant, get us the hell out of here!"

"We're working on it!" Grant shouted in response to Luke's demand.

Grant kept replaying the scenario. He would never have believed the metal grate moving into place, blocking the exit, if he hadn't witnessed it himself. It had moved from within the side of the well and slid across, covering the opening.

Then it had stopped, locking in place within a few seconds, creating the seemingly impenetrable barrier.

"Grant!" Craig cried in alarm.

The water rose to the top of the grate, then above it. Grant's heart raced in desperation as he watched Claire and Luke sink below its depths. He pounded at the metal, "No!"

A rushing of air filled the church. The water started receding.

CHAPTER THREE

Freezing and choking on frigid water, Claire tried to fill her lungs with air one last time before the water overtook them.

The deafening sound of rushing water disappeared, replaced with the pounding beat of her own heart. Strong arms wrapped around her body. She thanked the universe she wasn't alone. *Just let it come.* She felt the heroic man who was attempting to save her tense. Her heart broke. His hands moved to her waist, pulling her against him. Her eyes opened, the cold air hit her face, and she gasped for air. Confused and panicked by her swirling surroundings, she reached for something to grasp.

Her hero's arm restrained her, yelling in her ear. "Hang on to me!"

They impacted against the walls of the well twice before being sucked beneath the water again. The strong current swept them along. Claire clung to her hero's arms and prayed for it to be over. Cold air and a brutal jerk of her arm snapped her eyes open. Open air, trees, and a hundred-foot drop pushed all the air from her lungs.

"I've got you!" he shouted, getting her attention. One hand wrapped around a jutting rock, the other had a tight grip on her jacket.

"Um, okay," Claire said in a desperate attempt to focus her throbbing adrenaline-fueled consciousness.

Not dead, yet. Still close, but not dead

"Claire," he called.

She realized she had zoned out.

"Look to my left."

She obeyed, seeing a ledge a few feet within reach.

"I'm going to swing you over there. You are going to grab on."

"Yeah."

"You good?"

"Yeah, let's do it," Claire replied, summoning her inner bad-ass. Within a breath, she was swinging. Her body met the ledge and she grabbed at the rocks, rolling onto the shelf. Lying there, Claire's lungs expanded and oxygen entered her body. A surprisingly new sensation she'd always taken for granted. *Never again.*

Claire sat up, leaning against the wall, peering beyond the ledge. "We're under the waterfall."

"Looks like it," his deep voice said.

He made a few moves across the small expanse between the opening they'd fallen through and the rocky shelf. Looking at him, Claire's heart quivered a little. Dark short hair, deep brown eyes, chiseled features, and a muscular body his wet clothes did little to hide.

"You okay?" he asked.

He took in the sight of her, looking for any visible signs of injury from their experience. Claire Westin's thick brown hair was matted to her head. The icy water had blotched her porcelain skin. Her full pink lips were so perfect Luke found himself staring. Her eyes rose to meet his gaze. The crystal blue staring up at him made his heart skip a beat. An unexpected heat roared through his soul like the awakening of a Phoenix when she nodded.

Crap.

"Can we go back the way we came?" she asked, looking to the opening beside them.

The sound of metal grating on rock echoed out toward them. A large metal plate grinding into place covered the hole in the rockface. The exit they just barely escaped through sealed shut with a loud metal thud.

"Seriously?" Luke asked the universe.

"Kinda like Luke Skywalker in Empire. Down the chute we went . . ."

"The difference being we still have both hands and are not hanging upside down in outer-space."

"Feels cold enough," Claire said with a tremble.

"Adrenaline is wearing off," Luke replied, appreciating her witty reference and comeback. "We need to get moving while there's still light, but first we need to find a place to wring out our clothes."

"What?" Claire asked, her mouth gaping a little.

"We're wet, and the temperature is dropping. Wet clothes will suck the heat faster than damp clothes. We'll find an alcove or tree line, strip down, wring out our clothes of excess water and then put them back on. Once we reach the bottom, we can find a place for the night and start a fire."

"You're serious."

"Deadly. We're both at risk of hypothermia out here. It's not a solution, but it'll buy us some time."

"Who are you again?"

"Luke Melloy," he replied.

"Makes complete sense," she replied "You are the Navy Seal Priest-Demonologist."

Luke smirked.

She continued. "Now you can add Spelunker to your list."

"Who's to say it wasn't already on the list? I'm a big fan of spelunking. Invigorating sport."

"Good point." A lopsided smile edged Claire's lip.

Luke's heart raced. Her smile igniting a flame he'd thought had died long ago.

Luke pointed in the direction they needed to go. Claire led, setting the pace. They cut off from the natural path at the first tree line. Claire moved into the depth of the forest. He stayed on the trail, back turned. From their surroundings, he guessed it would take at least two hours to reach the bottom of the waterfall. From there, they would estimate the direction of the church and the fastest way back up.

Following Claire, he couldn't help but feel the heat burning in his chest. Wet, cold, and he assumed exhausted, she didn't utter a peep of protest. Quite the opposite. Her pace down the face of the waterfall remained steady and focused. She took careful but confident strides, her body silhouette delicious, with the gentle swell of the chest and a curve at her hips. She wasn't some walking stick of skin.

Luke imagined the feel of her muscular legs straddling his lap, her smooth shoulders and back flexing in his arms.

Holy shit, what am I doing? What the hell is wrong with me?

His luck with the ladies had always been hit or miss. As a professional demonologist, his life was dangerous, enigmatic, and unpredictable. These factors didn't usually inspire hope or a stable living, each being necessary in the eyes of the world and of a woman looking for a partner. Instead of pining for something he could never have, he stood aside, gaping at the wonder of the species. He had immense respect for women. Their amazing ability to not only live but thrive always astounded and intimidated him. *Men live. They get it done and make it work. Women get it done and have an impact.*

"Your turn," she said. Luke turned, taking in her shivering form.

"The exercise will help," he offered before moving into the woods himself. Stripping off his clothes, emptying his pockets, and removing his weapon, he made a little pile on a nearby stump. While wringing out his clothes, he recounted all the items waiting on the stump — nine-millimeter gun fully loaded, a standard utility knife, magnesium stick, wallet, dead cell phone. Luke redressed, starting to formulate a plan to get them through the night. Hopefully, Claire could push through until they found shelter.

He rejoined her on the path, and they started again. After a few moments of silence, Claire glanced at him. "You've been spelunking?"

"Yeah, once or twice," he replied, glad to see the cold hadn't affected her thinking — yet — and how she walked in stride with him instead of ahead.

"Do tell."

"I went last year with a buddy of mine to Mexico. We got into the lower levels of Crystal Cave."

"I thought Crystal Cave was only open to scientists?"

"He is dating one of the lead researchers."

"Nice, what was it like?"

"Incredible. Indescribable, a million crystal shards waiting for the sun," he said, noticing her intent focus on his face. Feeling scrutinized, he cleared his throat. "Have you ever been?"

"No, I'm a chicken. I saw a movie about the spelunking team getting stuck underground, and I hyperventilated. No way I could cope with the real deal," she said, shaking her head. "There's one cave I'd like to visit, although I don't think it is considered spelunking."

"What cave?"

"It's in Vietnam. I'm not sure of the name."

"Hang Son Doong?"

"Yes, that's the one. It has an independent ecosystem," Claire's face lit up with a smile. "I've only seen pictures, but it looks amazing."

"Have you ever heard of the Thrihnukagigur volcano?"

"I don't think so. Where is it?"

"Iceland."

"You can go spelunking into a volcano?"

"A dormant volcano."

"That helps clarify," she replied. "I'll admit the heat of a volcano sounds awesome right now."

After about an hour of walking, Claire's movements slowed, and he judged their position. Almost at the bottom. The escalating sound of the roaring waterfall meant they were close. Claire stumbled forward.

"Whoa!" Luke reached out to help. She steadied herself against a tree. "How are you doing?"

"Apparently in need of a break," she replied, the edge of a wistful smile shining in her lips.

"We're almost at the bottom."

"Just in time. The sun is going down."

"Grant is going to have people looking for us," Luke said.

"Too bad I forgot to stick my flare gun in my pocket this morning. My bad."

Luke couldn't help but laugh.

"Thank you, by the way."

"For?"

"For jumping into a well to try and save me and then actually saving me from a horrid death at the bottom of a waterfall," she replied, her cheeks reddening slightly.

"Thank me when we're out of here."

"I'm thanking you just in case we don't get out of here," she replied, her tone and eyes deathly serious.

It was the second sign of utter exhaustion Luke had seen since they'd escaped the well. Hollow cheeks, bloodshot eyes, and a tinge of blue in her lips made Luke's stomach drop. He needed to get her warm sooner rather than later.

"Do you think you can walk a little further?" Luke asked, and Claire nodded.

"Our estimation is the well, including the chute, is fifty to a hundred feet long. Once the water exits the well, the chute would have theoretically emptied somewhere east of Crest-water Falls." The local sheriff, Marty Mingus, pointed to a laminated map of the surrounding area.

"What's the problem?" Grant asked.

"The problem is the trail leading from here to the falls was washed out during the summer rains. To get to the falls on foot, we would need to go around. It's potentially an eight-hour hike in the best conditions."

"We don't have eight hours. Both Claire and Luke are soaked. While Luke is a survival expert, the temperatures are dropping. We have no idea about their resources."

"If your man is an ex-navy seal, he'll be somewhat pre-pared," the sheriff replied.

"Hopefully, but not for a long-term engagement. There's no way to know their injuries or if they are even—" Grant said.

"Don't say it, don't even think it," Craig said sternly, and Pip whimpered beside him. "They're gonna make it back. Both of them."

"Positive thoughts aside, I'm sending a helicopter up now to search before dusk settles in and we lose the sun. If we don't find them tonight, there's no way to search in the dark. Our best bet is to wait until morning. They just need to make it through the night," the sheriff stated plainly.

"It doesn't feel right not doing anything," Craig said.

"There is nothing we can do," Grant replied.

Grant sent the team back to the hotel for the night. There wouldn't be any ghost hunting until Luke and Claire were found safe. He waited to make a dreaded phone call to Claire's father, the CEO and founder of Westin Media group. Despite the rumor mill's insisting Albert Westin was a cut-throat politically powerful businessman, Grant found him always gracious and accommodating. Grant sometimes wondered if it was because his daughter was also always present at the meetings they'd had. He feared he was about to find out.

Dialing a direct line to Albert Westin, Grant listened to the phone ring.

"Hello?"

"Mr. Westin?"

"This is him. Who is this? How did you get this number?"

"This is Grant Henley, sir. I'm the founder of *Finders*. I work with and am a friend of your daughter Claire," Grant explained, praying the man had a good memory.

"Yes, Henley," Albert Westin said. "How can I help you?"

Grant explained the current situation, leaving out some of the obscure details. He detailed the search and rescue plans per the sheriff. The man listened calmly, not demanding or interrupting. When Grant finally took a breath, he waited for Westin to say something.

"Is there anything else?"

"No, sir. I've told you everything we know at this point."

"Thank you for calling me. Please keep me apprised of the developing situation."

"Yes, sir."

"Goodnight."

"Goodnight."

Grant stood digesting the short conversation. Not sure what to think or do, he walked back to the front of the church, where the sheriff stood talking to his deputy. The sheriff's phone buzzed. Grant watched him glance at it in confusion. He answered the call, immediately looking at Grant with accusing eyes.

Grant watched the sheriff talk, pace, and nod. The conversation ended. The man promptly walked to Grant. "Who the hell did you call?"

"Why?"

"Because the governor doesn't have me on speed-dial. He wanted a full update on our missing pair of ghost hunters," Mingus replied. "How the hell did he even know?

"I called Claire's father."

"Who the hell is her father?"

"Albert Westin."

The man's face paled, and he visibly gulped.

Even in a hick town like Crestwater, the name Albert Westin got a reaction.

Exhaustion was just about to usurp any will Claire had to move forward when salvation hit in the form of a deep cave. Luke told her to wait just outside while he checked it out. Claire was not going to argue. She didn't think she could take another step. The uncontrolled shivering was getting annoying. Luke said it was her body's way of generating heat. Her tense muscles felt like they'd turned to ice. She needed to melt. She leaned against the rock wall, scanning their surroundings as the sun started its descent against the horizon. Trees, plants, leaves on the ground, dirt, and rocks—aka the extent of her wilderness vocabulary.

Luke, she guessed, could identify each type of everything and how long they could survive off it. Ever since he'd swung her over onto the ledge, Claire knew she was safe with him. If someone would've said *you will face a life or death struggle — oh, by the way, there will be an extremely handsome navy seal there to help you along* — she would not only have laughed but had them tested for drugs.

Adventures were not her thing. Her thing was supplying the money for *others* to go on the adventure, record it, and bring it back for her to make money. Being the one in the middle of the action was mind-blowing. Thank God there were no cameras.

Her mind flitted back to the church and the well. Had she let her imagination run away with her, and this was all a big accident? Could there be a logical explanation? It didn't feel right. Nothing felt right.

"Claire?"

The sound of his voice brought her back. A small burst of warmth through her body lifted her off the rock. "I'm here."

He walked out of the dark cave with a smile. "I think we're good to go."

Claire followed him inside, he offered her a rock to sit on, she gladly accepted. "Rest here while I get to work on a fire. No sleeping."

"Got it," she replied with a nod. After a few minutes of continual shivering, she was finding that one request much harder than she'd ever imagined. The need to close her eyes and go into the warm darkness pulled on her repeatedly. She stood up and paced to comply with his instructions.

Luke returned quickly with kindling, a few more significant pieces, and tree brush. Within moments there was a crackling fire. She moved toward the warmth like a moth to a flame.

"Before you get comfortable, I need you to do something," Luke said, his eyes questioning.

She dreaded his request. Ten minutes later, she returned to the fire, panties and bra in hand. Seeing a pair of boxers and a gray t-shirt hung on a makeshift rack a few feet above the heat of the fire, she carefully hung her garments to dry. Undergarments were to dry first so that when the rest of the clothing came off to dry, they would have something to wear while they waited.

Could be interesting

Claire settled in next to the fire, wanting to roll around in the warmth of the flames. Still shivering, she shifted slightly every few minutes like a chicken on a spit, wanting to warm every side of her body, not just the front. Her butt tingled and itched, but she resisted the need to heat it for fear of looking like a complete idiot.

Luke wandered in and out of the cave. The light from outside grew dimmer by the minute. He brought in armfuls of leaves, piling them up on the opposite side of where she sat, near the wall of the cave, glancing in her direction every so often. Claire assumed that was to make sure she hadn't dozed off. As she watched his repeated work on their survival, the guilt of all his manual labor weighed on her.

"Do you need some help?" Claire asked.

He dumped the latest pile of leaves onto the stack. "Nope, you get warm. That's all I need you to do right now."

His tone, although reassuring, struck her the wrong way. She was not helpless. She could contribute to their well-being. Who put him in charge anyway? Technically, she was his boss. Claire couldn't stand the thought of him thinking she was a helpless girl. She lifted herself off the ground, walking to the mouth of the cave.

"What are you doing?"

"We are going to need more wood for the fire. I'm going out to find some."

"No, you're not," he said, stepping in front of her.

"Yes, I am," she said, attempting to move around him.

He blocked her again. "Claire, while I appreciate you wanting to help, I need you to go back and sit down."

"This is ridiculous. I'm not a child!"

"Are you still shivering?"

"Yes, it's cold."

"No, *you* are cold."

"What?"

"Your body temperature is hovering around ninety-three degrees right now," he said.

Claire started to object but couldn't.

"Thus, your shivering is your body's attempt to prevent your core body temperature from dropping below ninety degrees. If your core temperature drops below ninety degrees, you will go into hypothermic shock and most likely die. There are five stages of hypothermia. You were on the cusp of stage two when we arrived in the cave. The only reason you are still conscious is that you are sitting in front of that fire shivering. So, for God's sakes, please go sit down so I can finish prepping for the cold night ahead."

Claire's face fell, making her look like a scolded puppy.
Luke watched her walk to the fire, taking a seat. He felt slightly guilty, as he'd exaggerated just a tad, but he was genuinely worried about her health and the night ahead of them. She'd been in the cold water much longer. It was logical to assume her core temperature was indeed lower. He guessed he was at a balmy ninety-six. He always ran hot, with a regular temp of ninety-nine. Half his size and in the water twice as long meant she was at ninety-three or below.

Two more trips for leaves and they should be good. It wasn't going to be a five-star hotel, but it would trap the warmth and offer a small cushion against the cold rock beneath their feet. The search for kindling and leaves was mindless. Luke kept trying to find the best way to broach the needed next step in the night's plan. They were going to need to strip to dry their clothes. Body heat would be their best bet. Drying their undergarments was a strategic move. He'd wanted to provide as much ease in an uncomfortable situation as he could.

They wouldn't be completely naked laying beneath the leaves together. He worried about any physical reactions from being close to Claire. The responses would be completely unintentional, of course. He had no desire to do anything but get warm, but he couldn't deny the growing attraction, magnetism he hadn't felt since before he joined the seals — unexpected, inopportune, and inappropriate. She was, in fact, his boss, a new colleague, and the friend of his best friend. The situation could become very complicated very quickly. Yet all these reasons would not stop his chest from warming every time she looked at him.

Feeling like a wounded animal and acting like a spoiled child wasn't going to help anyone. Staring into the fire and becoming acutely aware of her lace underwear hanging just a few feet away, Claire tucked her ego away and willed the fire's heat into her pores.

After a little while, Luke returned to the cave for good and appeared in the light of the fire. He retrieved his boxers off the branch, testing them. He then reached out to her lace panties and bra. His rough hand grasped the fabric without restraint. The image sent a tingle up Claire's spine, and she squelched a gasp.

"All good," Luke said, meeting her eyes. "I'll change first."

She nodded, licking her lips in apprehension. *Stop it, Claire. We are in a life-threatening situation. There is nothing sexual about this scenario at all.* Claire chewed on her thumb. Luke reappeared. Shirtless, his muscle-bound hard body almost made her woozy. A gold chain holding a gleaming gold cross reminded her of the faith and fire beyond his body. The fact that he was walking with hesitation as if she would in any way be appalled by his semi-nakedness made her cheeks warm. He stood silent. His gaze locked with hers.

Look away, look away — look somewhere else!

"Your turn," he said with a lopsided grin.

Claire could've sworn she saw a little pink rise above his chiseled cheekbones. She nodded, grabbing her clothes.

"Claire, wait."

Wait — what — why wait — I need to escape before I explode.
"Take this as well," he said, handing her his t-shirt.
"Won't you need it?"
"I'd rather you wear it."
"But I . . ."
"Please?"
His eyes pleaded, and she couldn't refuse.

Their hands brushed while exchanging the shirt. A swirl of tingles lit up Claire's body. "Thanks."

Claire moved off to the right. Luke forced himself to not look in her direction, giving her needed privacy. Arranging his clothes to dry, he left a drying rod for Claire's things.

You're a professional. Your attraction to this woman is superficial and based on the extreme circumstances of the moment. Nothing more. Focus.

Luke turned to the bed of leaves. Realizing his little pep talk wasn't working, he ran a frustrated hand over the back of his neck. Claire stepped into his line of sight, and he stopped. Her hair, once pulled up and away from her face, had turned into a cascade of caramel dancing in the firelight. She moved carefully, her bare feet unsteady on the rocky floor. The edge of his gray t-shirt showed off her long toned legs but covered enough to tweak his imagination. Her blue eyes shone brightly, despite the surrounding darkness. Luke struggled to focus on anything but the ravishing beauty walking toward him.

"Where do you want me to put these?" she asked, her eyes full of uncertainty.

"I'll . . ." he started and stopped, recalling her need not to be coddled. "You can hang them there." He pointed to the piece of wood hanging over the fire.

She stepped forward. Luke put another log on the fire and moved to the pile of leaves.

"How is this gonna work?" she asked, her gentle voice a small whisper from behind.

"The idea is to create heat through mutual body warmth, then trap the heat under the leaves to raise body temperature. Not the most ideal situation, but it's all we have until the clothes dry out," Luke said.

Claire was already shivering violently. He wasted no more time.

"You're going to lie down first, on your side facing the wall. I'll lie down next to you, cover you with my body as much as possible. Once settled in, we can cover ourselves with the leaves."

Claire went from feeling awkward to not caring one single bit about her nakedness. She was freaking cold! She moved forward, the sharp rocks beneath her feet making her wince in pain. Reaching the glossy leaves was a comfort for her feet. She lowered first to her knees, then bent forward on her hands. She was shifting to get comfortable as possible, finding herself struggling without something beneath her head.

The sound of rustling and the delicious warmth of his body alerted Claire to Luke's presence. His large arm slid beneath her neck to cradle her head, and she thanked God for miracles. Her body shivered in response. Luke started twisting, and she could feel him draping the leaves over their bodies. Once finished, his free arm wrapped securely around her waist, pulling her solidly against his heated chest. If she would stop shivering, she could almost feel sleep pulling her away.

"No sleeping, princess."

"No promises."

"Not an option."

"Fine," she said. "Princess?"

"Sorry, something I call my niece."

Claire didn't know whether to be offended or enamored. She decided she didn't care as long as he didn't move.

"I apologize in advance for any physical reactions I may have to this situation."

The comment made her smile for both the acknowledgment and the admission.

"I apologize in advance for any shifting, rubbing, or pressure I may cause in making it worse," she offered and could almost feel his smile at her neck.

There was a long silence. Claire felt herself drifting off slightly.

"No sleeping," he whispered gently, catching her in the act. The man's timing was impeccable.

"If you want me to stay awake, you're going to have to talk to me, hero."

"I can do that. Just don't call me that, please."

"What? Hero?"

"Yes."

"Why?"

"It's just not a term I'm comfortable with," he replied softly.

"Noted," Claire replied, and she focused on the rise and fall of his chest against her back. "How did you meet Grant?"

"I served with Grant's brother for six years. We met after he passed."

"I'm sorry," Claire gulped back her inner beratement, feeling the tension in his body. "Did he die in the line of duty?"

"Yes," Luke replied, his voice low and gruff. "How did you meet Grant?"

"At a Ghost Hunting convention. We exchanged information, and about a year later we premiered *Finders* on Sci-Fi."

"Sci-Fi?"

"The Science-Fiction television network," she replied. "You really are out of the media loop. Grant said you're a bit of a hermit."

"Did he now? What else did Grant tell you about me?" Luke asked with a small laugh.

Claire's body relaxed.

"Lots of things, I have your entire resume on my desk. Grant fought hard to make you part of this team."

"Fought hard with who?"

"Himself, I think."

"What do you mean?"

"Well, I have no say in who Grant adds or removes from the *Finders* team."

"You're not my boss?" Luke asked.

Claire stifled a giggle.

"Well, hell, I'm freezing my ass off for nothing," Luke replied, and she laughed aloud. His arm tightened around her, pulling her closer to him, and she wondered if the action was conscious or unconscious.

"I get the navy seals thing, obviously," Claire said. "What about the demonology — priest segue?"

"I thought you had my full bio?"

"I have the what and the when but not the why and how."

"Those are two short questions with lengthy answers."

"We have all night," she replied and after a long silence wondered if he was going to answer.

"I knew from an early age I was meant to work in the service of the Lord," Luke started, his voice low and a bit strained. "For a kid raised in a Catholic family, the calling meant the priesthood. I graduated from high school, did a couple of years in college, and then went to Seminary. I did everything to fulfill my calling."

"It wasn't enough?"

"The priesthood is very rewarding in its respect, but there

was still a tugging for more. I didn't know what it meant, but something didn't feel right. I started to feel the weight of the political ramifications of religion. I wasn't completely on board with what the Catholic Church had in mind for me. I took a leave of absence and joined the seals."

"It's quite a change."

"The decision gave a couple people whiplash," Luke said, the warmth of a smile in his voice. "I needed something physical, something more than my brain, something outside theology, and I still wanted to help people."

"Did you find what you were looking for?"

"For the most part, yes. I found more than I expected."

"How so?"

"My life in the navy was the most physically challenging, mentally clarifying, soul rewarding experience of my life thus far. It is also the vehicle that showed me my true path."

"Something happened while you were a seal, making you decide to become a demonologist?"

"I witnessed my first exorcism as a seal. It was then I knew what I needed to do," Luke replied. "I knew why I'm here. What God was calling me to do."

"To fight demons?" Claire said before thinking, then shifted to face him in regret. "I didn't mean that disrespectfully at all . . ."

The worry in her eyes that she had somehow offended him with the question brought a small smile to his lips. They were so close he could feel the brush of her breath on his chin. "No offense taken," Luke said, the urge to lean forward and kiss her causing his breath to deepen in his effort to control.

Claire lay staring up at him as if wanting to confirm he was telling the truth before rolling her head away. Luke exhaled.

Crisis averted.

"You believe in demons?" Claire asked, a hint of hesitation

in her voice.

"Yes."

"Have you ever seen one?"

"Yes," Luke said, then felt her body stiffen a little against him. He wondered was it out of fear or excitement. He decided it was getting a bit too serious and was tired of the focus of their conversation on him. "Have you ever seen a Demon?"

"Once, although I'm not sure it was an actual Demon," Claire replied.

Luke's head jerked up in shock. "What happened exactly?" Luke asked.

"I was walking in the middle of a field with Pip a few years ago. I remember the sun shining down. It was a hot day. Something blocked the sun's light. I turned toward the shadow. Standing in the distance was a large hooded figure. I couldn't see a face, but I knew it was looking at me."

"Then what happened?"

"I woke up on the ground with Pip licking my face. I'll admit at the time I figured it was heatstroke, but now, I'm not so sure." Claire shrugged her shoulders.

"What changed your mind?"

"Today," Claire replied, turning toward him. "Luke, I didn't just fall down a well—someone or something pushed me."

CHAPTER FOUR

The heat on his back from the fire dwindled. Luke reluctantly shifted to rise from the cocoon of warmth. It was far from perfect, but sufficient none-the-less.

The small brush of Claire's hand caused his temperature to rise exponentially. Covering her in leaves, he rose from their nest of warmth to check the clothes and add kindling to the fire. Claire's clothes were almost dry. His clothes were still a little damp but nothing he couldn't ignore.

"How are we looking, chief?"

"Good. About another hour, and we can get dressed," Luke said, stoking the flames back up to a gentle crackle.

"I'm not shivering anymore, thanks to our makeshift leaf nest thing. Would it be okay for me to sleep, maybe?" Claire asked, watching him move back into position beside her.

"I don't see why not. We can shift positions if you'd like so you are facing the fire." Luke watched her ponder the option for a moment.

She rose to her feet, stepping over him. Luke had to readjust the pile of leaves, but once Claire lay down, he pulled her close. She laid her head on his arm. His mind flashed *ownership*.

"How do you fight a Demon?" Claire asked. The previous conversation had changed and morphed into funny stories about Grant and his brother Daniel. Though Luke hadn't forgotten in any way what Claire had stated, he just wasn't sure how to respond. It wasn't a matter of belief. He believed her completely. He just needed more information. Claire bringing demons up again reinforced his opinion. Someone or something had attacked her in the church.

"Tell me about the church," Luke replied.

"I caught the story by accident. The church—most well known as, get this, the Smoldering Beacon of Wyoming—is infamous for its extinguishment of the witch population in the late 1800s."

"Charming."

"Reverend Walter Channing built up a league of followers whose sole purpose was finding witches so they could be executed here at the Crestwater Church. Reverend Channing believed with each soul of the witch population cleansed, he and his followers became closer to God."

"Explains the booby-trapped well," Luke said.

"I guess it does, although I'm pretty sure he burnt the witches, not drowned," Claire replied, twirling a loose strand of her honey-brown hair around her finger. "Anyway, fast forward to the present day. Teenager Kelsey James visits the church on a dare with her boyfriend, Matt something-or-other. He hears a noise in the back of the church, goes to check it out, comes back, and Kelsey is gone. He searches for her, finds her laughing on the other side of the church, and takes her home safe and sound. The next morning Kelsey's father reports her missing to the local Sheriff's department. After an eighteen-hour search, they found her in the church."

"Was it a prank?" Luke asked, feeling slightly guilty for doubting the teen's story.

"A question is still up for debate. However, when the police found Kelsey, she is said to have been in a catatonic state, immobile, incoherent, and unresponsive. Either the girl should teach a master class on trauma, or she experienced something so awful she's hiding in her mind from it," Claire said.

"She is why you brought *Finders* to Crestwater? To find the truth?"

"Yeah, and the media buzz surrounding the story is going to boost our ratings substantially."

"It's about the money?" Luke shifted, unsure of how to react to her response.

"No, it's about finding the truth, whatever we can prove," Claire said. "It's also a perfect opportunity for *Finders* to make their mark in the paranormal playing field, which will mean more opportunities for everyone."

"Meaning, it's about supply and demand, creating the opportunity, creating the demand, thus the increase in return on your investment," Luke said, keeping his voice steady and non-accusatory.

"Yes and no," Claire replied. "Why can't it be about both?"

"Explain."

"When Grant came to me with his vision for *Finders,* it was one of education, adventure, knowledge, experience, and growth. His goal is to help people who are afflicted by paranormal activity. The best way to help people is to educate them about the paranormal. *Finders* works to show both sides. We show the pipes banging against the walls when it is cold and the rocking chair moving of its own accord. In either scenario, we're showing people the truth."

Claire spoke with the conviction of a parent. "I invested in *Finders* because of his vision. The more exposure *Finders* has, the more demand I create, the more people we can help. I'm not going to say the money doesn't have anything to do with it. It does. The money we make funds the trips and hotel stays, the equipment, the editing, the marketing, everything. Without the money, we would be piling up VHS tapes in a garage. We're not. We're in Wyoming, freezing our butts off to help uncover the truth for a small town."

"I didn't mean to doubt your intention or sound patronizing. If it came across that way, I apologize," Luke said.

"Apology accepted but not needed," Claire replied. "Defending *Finders* is a hot button of mine. I seem to have to do it regularly."

"If it's any consolation, you do an excellent job."

"Thanks," she said, her body relaxing into his length. "You never did answer my question."

"Which one?"

"How do you fight a Demon?"

"With faith."

Their clothing finished drying just after midnight. Luke and Claire redressed. Curling back into their leaf bed to sleep, and despite exhaustion wanting to take over his body, Luke's mind whirled like a kicked hornet's nest.

What was he doing here, running?

No, it was clear why he was here. An innocent needed him. Claire needed him.

Was he jumping to conclusions? In truth, he didn't know Claire, but there was something about this woman he was drawn to, a pull he didn't recognize. Whether it would remain strong or dissipate once they returned to reality, he didn't know. At this moment he didn't care. He held onto the feeling, the warmth of her body beside him, the scent of her hair, the calmness of her face, memorizing every inch of Claire Westin. If this moment was all he would have, it would be enough to last him a lifetime.

He would take it in, savor it, and then hide it in the back of his mind. They could never be. It was the only way to protect her.

Too early to return to the church and unable to sleep, Grant paced his room until the rug started to look worn. Pip sat curled at the foot of the bed, eyes alert and imploring. When Grant sat motionlessly, unable to stop his mind from spinning out of control with endless scenarios, Pip lay at his feet as if experiencing the same struggles and anxiety about his master.

They were early to meet Craig.

They arrived at the church to see dawn break over the horizon. Several sheriff's cars were parked directly in front, barricading the entrance. The area was taped off. Sheriff Mingus and his deputies were talking with two other men in police jackets. Grant recognized the equipment and general stance of the reporting media members. Somehow the story had leaked. Now the whole world wanted to know what happened. He wondered if Albert Westin had anything to do with their quick appearance.

Grant and Craig walked toward the tape to be immediately swarmed by the various media teams, shouting random incoherent questions. They walked through them in silence, ducked under the tape, and joined the sheriff and his team by the church doors.

"Good morning, gentlemen. I see the pestilence of the day has greeted you."

"Sure have," Grant replied. "What's the plan?"

"We have two helicopters ready to go. I was planning on having one of you in each bird to help in the search. Does that work for you?"

"Yeah, that works," Grant said.

Craig nodded his consent and at the same moment a sigh of relief left Grant's lungs. He'd feared the sheriff would cut them out of the search due to the pressure from the governor, but apparently he'd chosen to embrace their assistance. Thank God.

"I just reviewed their estimated position with the pilots. We're going to start here," Mingus said, pointing to the laminated map from the previous evening. "We'll work in two circles, east and west. The exit point for the tunnel we postulated is here. If your team was able to withdraw from the tunnel safely, they would have two options. One to climb up and over, or option two, down and then up. The flight plan covers both scenarios. Hopefully, we will catch a break and find them sooner rather than later. Weather is gonna be brisk. The winds are supposed to be bad this afternoon, which will ground the copters."

"When do we leave?"

"They're ready when you are," Mingus replied with a nod.

"Let's go."

Claire finished stomping out the fire and said farewell to the cave. Taking one last look at the small area, she took a mental snapshot before moving out toward the sun.

Luke waited, stretching his back.

"Nothing like a rock bed to put a crick in your neck," Claire said.

"You got that right."

"I'll personally pay for your massage when we get back to civilization," she offered, genuinely feeling bad about the situation.

"There's no need. I'm fine," Luke replied, his voice low and cold. "You ready to head out?"

"Yeah, let's go."

Luke raised his hand for her to take the lead. Claire followed the path downward in silence. The rushing of water from the river flowing away from the waterfall created a deafening white noise. The sun's beams were warm, but the air was cold. Dry clothing made all the difference. Her stomach grumbled in protest. Thinking back to her last meal, Claire realized she hadn't eaten since lunch the previous day.

"Do you think it would be okay to drink from the river?"

she asked.

"Should be fine," Luke replied. "Just be careful not to slip and fall in."

"So not funny," Claire said with a grin.

"I'm not kidding," he replied, his face stoic and withdrawn.

A chill climbed up Claire's spine. She turned away, ignoring the pang in her chest. Moving slowly down the bank to the side of the river, she cursed her shoes for their lack of traction and would swear her fury to the heavens if she did fall in. She steadied herself at the edge, digging her feet into the mud oozing around her shoes. Bending into a squat, she cupped her hands, dipping them into the water. She took a sip. The water was cold but refreshing. Losing her balance, a little, she adjusted and made a mental note to work on her body strength and do more squats when she got back to the gym.

Determined to not look at Luke, she wondered if she'd done anything to offend him. Maybe he wasn't a morning person. An unearthly shiver ran up her spine. She shook it off, her gaze going to the water spilling over the rocks. The sight was violent and beautiful in the same breath. Something odd caught her eye, white beneath the clear water. A bleached rock? Adjusting her focus, she shifted. The object became clear. She looked away. Her breath caught in her throat. She saw another. She gasped in horror, her brain processing the images. Skulls — two skulls lay at her feet beneath the water of the river.

The water she had drunk.

Bile rose in her throat, burning the back of her mouth.

Turning, she expelled the contents of her stomach.

"Claire!"

She heard him calling to her but couldn't move. It seemed mere seconds before Luke's hand was on her shoulder, his eyes wide in concern.

Luke moved to better see what she was doing. He'd watched her lose her balance and then turn in distress. He'd called out her name. When she didn't respond, his stomach clenched. Luke jogged toward the river's edge. Confused as to what had happened, he scanned the area and found nothing. Reaching her, he placed a hand on her shoulder.

She turned, her eyes welling with tears, her face drawn and pale.

"What happened?"

"I drank the water," Claire replied.

Luke struggled to comprehend. "What?"

"Oh, God," Claire said, rising from her squatting position, wiping her hand across her nose. "They must've died here. They were drowned and dropped into the river. No one would have ever known."

"Claire, you're not making any sense," Luke said, taking her by the shoulders. "Who died?"

She hesitated, staring deep into his eyes, her face pensive and tense. "There are bodies in the river."

"What?"

"I saw at least two skulls," she said, her breath coming in waves.

"Where?" Luke asked, and Claire pointed. "Stay here. Do not move."

Claire nodded, wiping at her nose again.

Luke left her to investigate. It took him a few minutes, but once he saw the first skull, he then saw a second and a third, putting it together in his head. The well, the waterfall, he understood. They were in a graveyard, and she had drunk the water.

His stomach clenched just thinking about it, but he pushed

the revulsion away, knowing there was nothing wrong with the water. In a running river, the flesh of the bodies had washed away years ago. The bone was as clean as the rocks surrounding it. The thought of it, though, was revolting.

Quickly returning to Claire, she looked at him in question. "You saw them?"

"Yes."

"I didn't imagine it?"

"No," Luke said.

Claire seemed to get paler.

"Let's get out of here."

Claire nodded. He helped her up the ridge and back to the path. She stood a moment, looking fragile and worn. Luke stepped forward, pulling her into a hug.

"I didn't think this could get any more awful."

"It's okay. It's over," Luke said.

"How many did you see?"

"More than two."

"Oh, God it's awful," she said, burrowing against his chest.

"It is, but we found them. Now we can lay their souls to rest and maybe find them a little justice."

Claire pulled back, looking up into his eyes. "You're right."

Having her in his arms felt good. It felt right. He didn't want to let go. That was a problem. A big problem.

The sound of whirring metal caught their attention. They looked up. A helicopter came into view above the trees. They jumped and waved. The aircraft circled once and came back around.

"Do they see us?" Claire asked.

"Looks like it."

"What do we do now?"

"We wait and watch for where they land," Luke said.

They waited, and as predicted, the helicopter landed in a clearing to their left about three-hundred yards from them.

Luke looked at Claire, ready to meet their rescue party. Claire turned into him, pressing her lips against his in a kiss. The electricity coming off her body was beyond enthralling. All the doubts he'd had about himself, her, or their purpose disappeared. Overwhelmed, Luke drank it in like a man in the desert in need of water.

She pulled away before he had a chance to react, her smile wide and bright before she jogged to the helicopter.

Luke took a deep breath and followed.

Claire was already in the helicopter when he arrived. Grant stood with an outstretched hand.

"You don't look too worse for wear," Grant said, shaking his hand enthusiastically.

"Good to see you too, brother," Luke replied.

"Let's go."

"Wait, we have a problem," Luke said, quickly explaining their discovery at the river. "Can we drop a marker here so the authorities can come back with a forensic team?"

Grant walked around and talked to the pilot, who gave a thumbs up, and Grant returned. "He said he would make a note of the coordinates and give them to us when we land. We can pass the info onto the sheriff. Let's go!"

The helicopter lifted off. Grant pondered the news of a graveyard below them. There was a story there, and he would get more details from Luke and Claire after they'd been checked out. Looking across at his friends, he released a long breath of relief. They looked a little worse for wear. He'd noticed a brief exchange just before Claire boarded the helicopter and made a mental note to ask Luke about it at a later time. They were alive, and that was what mattered.

Fifteen minutes to the church, and Grant was still awed by the wilderness below. They were lucky to have found Claire and Luke when they did. He said a small prayer of thanks. Upon their approach, he noticed the swarm of media had grown. Luke looked to him in confusion. "Media got wind of what happened. Welcome to show business."

Grant helped Claire out of the helicopter. They immediately moved to a caravan of ambulances. Within moments, something brushed Grant's arm. He turned to see someone tackle Claire to the ground. He grabbed at the shoulders of the person to pull them off, to no avail. Luke, beside him, attempted to do the same. A blow to his chest threw Grant back. He landed fifteen yards away, the wind knocked out of him. He struggled to breathe, finally recovered, and rushed back to the struggle. Luke had the assailant in a sleeper hold. After a few moments of effort, they collapsed to the ground. Luke scooped Claire into his arms, taking her to the nearby ambulance. Sheriff's deputies surrounded the aggressor. Grant moved toward the ambulance, catching sight of the unconscious attacker. It was a teenage girl.

Kelsey James?

Claire just wanted to sleep, but they insisted on poking and prodding her aching body. Every muscle, every pore of her existence was in agony from her tingling toes to the muscles in her neck. It all screamed *enough!*

Wasn't I really tempting fate with the whole I didn't think it could get any worse *thing? Holy crap all I need now is to get struck by lightning, and I'd have the trifecta!*

Everything after her gutsy move to kiss Luke was a complete blur. It was all too much to sort through. She didn't have the energy or the will to care. There was a knock. The door to the room creaked a little as it opened. Grant and Luke entered.

Claire shifted in the bed, very aware of the fact she hadn't looked in a mirror since first arriving at the church.

"Hey, beautiful," Grant said, moving to the bed and

kissing her on the cheek.

Luke hung back by the door, his eyes focused.

"Hey, guys," Claire attempted, but the words came out raspy and broken.

Grant took a seat on the bed across from her, holding her hand. "You scared the crap out of all of us, Claire. No more ghost hunting for you."

Claire smiled.

"How are you feeling?"

"Tired," Claire eked out, followed by a thumbs up. She motioned to Luke with a questioning expression.

"I'm good, a clean bill of health," Luke replied.

Claire immediately moved to get out of the bed. Grant shook his head and laughed. "Not so fast there, Tomb Raider. The doctor hasn't discharged you yet."

As if on cue there was another knock at the door. A doctor entered with a nod.

"We'll be right outside if you need us," Grant said, patting her hand before taking his exit with Luke.

A chill ran up Claire's spine. Her intake of air caused her to cough again.

"Please hold still," the doctor said while examining her neck.

Claire wanted to apologize but then thought better of it. She was thinking back to Luke standing in the background, keeping his distance. Then there was his odd behavior at the river before the discovery. Now they were back in the real world, did everything that had happened between them become somehow invalid? What happened in the cave stayed in the cave? Not much had happened, really. Just an undeniable feeling of warmth and security growing within her chest whenever he was near. What was it about him that made her lose her head? Her usual self-confident, professional but approachable demeanor melted like ice in a steaming cup of tea every time he came within speaking distance. Her heart fluttered, her stomach warmed, and her brain went from succinct and focused to flowery and enamored.

Claire wasn't a sucker for flights of romantic fancy. Which was why she'd kissed him before they left. The display of affection was very impromptu. She couldn't believe she'd pulled it off. No regrets. It was a stolen moment she would never forget.

The helpful nurse fluttered about assisting and taking notes. Claire half-listened, wanting Grant and Luke to return and not leave her alone with these people. The doctor asked her to follow a penlight. She did so with no problem. The light, however, caused her headache to spike and another chill enveloped her body.

The doctor moved on to the next phase of the examination. Claire coughed again, seeing a shadow from the corner of her eye. The shadow moved from her side to behind, the doctor looming over his shoulders. She squinted at the foggy silhouette. It grew in height and depth, slowly overtaking the room. Claire's body shook, her breaths coming in shallow fear-filled gasps.

"Ms. Westin, I need you to calm down."

"No, I need to leave. I want to leave, please," Claire said in a whisper, the anxiety of her visions paralyzing her lungs.

"Not until the examination is complete."

"Thank you, I'm fine," Claire insisted, moving off the bed despite the abrupt fuzziness edging her sight.

"Nurse, help me here," he said, grasping Claire's arms and preventing her from moving. "I'm going to give you a sedative to calm you down, so we can—a"

The shadowed presence took a solid form standing behind both the doctor and the nurse. Claire stopped hearing the doctor's prattle. A face appeared within the dark, hollow eyes and an open mouth. It reminded her of *The Screaming Man* painting. A deafening howl emanated from the dark figure. Claire's survival instincts took hold. She kicked the doctor out of the way, thrashing at the nurse and the cart of examination tools.

Claire bolted out of the room. Away from the shadows, but they followed. With no focus, she ran. Her blood pumping and heart racing, she could feel them all around her, pulling at her like a magnet pulling a piece of metal across the table. Each shadow's pull was a little different. Blind to anything but escape, she ran through the halls of the hospital. Seeing a doorway ahead, she lunged for it. The door opened. The shadows disappeared. Catching her breath, she leaned heavily against the closed door. Trying to make sense of what happened. Her temporary insanity? Had she hit her head? Did the lack of oxygen from her attacker's stranglehold around her neck do more damage than she realized? What was happening? What would cause these hallucinations?

Like a bursting water balloon, a flood of strange noises and images hit her mind's eye, dropping Claire to her knees. Her dull headache warped into a colossal migraine, threatening to rip her in half. She cried out, unable to hear her screams over the loud crashing in her mind.

"Claire."

The voice was distant but familiar. The noise lowered to a dull roar, and Claire opened her eyes.

"Claire."

Rising from her fetal position on the floor, Claire straightened her back looking for the source of the voice. Two sharp eyes stared at her with overpowering animosity, a crackle pierced from its grotesque mouth, resounding in an amused tone. Claire stood paralyzed, unable to move or look away. Wetness dampened her cheeks. Darkness emanated from the sight to wrap itself around her body.

Luke and Grant rounded the corner, hospital coffee in hand. Sherriff Mingus approached.

"Sheriff Mingus, nice to see you again," Grant greeted, shaking the man's hand. "Thanks again for all of your help the past few days."

"It's my pleasure. Just glad we got everyone back safe." He shook Grant's hand, looking to Luke, who extended his hand as well with a grateful nod. "I wanted to come by and give you an update on your discovery."

"Of course, thank you for keeping us in the loop," Luke said.

"It's the least I can do," he said. "A forensic anthropology team from DC is flying in to extract the remains and try and identify the cause of death, and anything else we can uncover."

"Are they optimistic, considering the condition of the bones?" Luke asked.

"According to the team lead, they love a challenge," he replied. "How is Ms. Westin?"

"She is doing well, all things considered. The doctors are checking her out right now," Grant replied. "How soon can we get back in the church?"

"I would give it a few days until the media buzz dies down," he answered with a nod.

"That works. We can move things around to other projects."

"You have other locations in the area to investigate?"

"Yes, a residence, and the Crestwater Library."

"I've been called to the library a few times over the years for reports of strange noises and whispers," the sheriff said with a smile. "It'll be interesting to see what you capture."

"We'll be happy to share anything we find."

"I need to get back to the station. Please, let Ms. Westin know we're all happy she's okay. Let me know if you need anything."

"Thanks again. We appreciate it," Grant said, shaking the man's hand once more before walking away.

"He's very cooperative," Luke commented.

"I think he is, and he's scared of Claire's Dad," Grant replied.

The men walked back to Claire's room and knocked on the door, "Why's that?"

"Well, I . . ." Grant stopped, seeing the doctor sitting on Claire's bed, rubbing the back of his head. "What happened?"

"Where's Claire?" Luke asked.

Luke's stomach clenched. He turned from the doorway, searching the hallway.

"Did you see which way she went?" Grant asked.

"To the left, I think," the nurse replied.

Grant looked at Luke. "I'll check the security cameras on the floor." He moved to the nurse's station.

Luke nodded, taking a deep, cleansing breath. He waited, calming his body and mind. "Claire."

He heard a voice call. Following the voice, he was led through the hallway. A prayer of guidance repeatedly played in his mind. Like a chant, he kept hearing her name. The rhythm hastened his steps, and he came to a door.

Luke hesitated, then pushed the door open. He didn't see anything in the darkened room. A chill stiffened his back when his breath became visible. Stepping inside, he found Claire standing just beside the door. A girl lay in the bed staring at him, watching his every movement. Her eyes were cold and calculating.

"Claire," he said softly, moving toward where she stood. The rolling bed table moved, pushing itself between himself and Claire. Luke forced himself not to react, then moved it out of the way. "Claire, shut it out. Whatever's happening, you can shut it out."

The door opened. Grant stepped into the room and asked, "What's happening?"

"I'm not sure," Luke replied, moving steadily toward Claire but motioning to the girl in the bed. "I need you to step into her line of sight but not look at her."

"Got it," Grant said, moving between Luke and the bed, facing the doorway. Luke immediately reached out for Claire's hand, wrapping it in his.

"Claire, can you hear me?" He glanced at the woman in the bed. He looked back. Claire blinked a few times, looking disoriented and confused.

"Luke?"

"Yeah," he replied, purposely blocking her view. "The doctor said enough visiting for the day. Let's go back to your room."

She nodded. Luke led her toward the door. Grant followed. They moved out into the hallway. Claire brushed a hand through her hair.

"Can you do me a favor?" Claire asked as they reached her room.

"Anything," Grant said.

"Can you make sure we get regular updates on Kelsey? I want to make sure she's being taken care of. Something didn't seem right when we were visiting. I'm worried about her, poor thing."

Luke's stomach twisted into a knot.

CHAPTER FIVE

She needed a hot bath to rid her of the chill enveloping her body, and a night of long, deep sleep. Claire arrived in her hotel room, immediately flipping on the light switch.

Everything was as she'd left it. A small sigh of relief escaped her chest. Pip rushed from the bedroom, looking at her eagerly. All her anxiety disappeared. She took a seat on the couch, allowing the dog to cover her with kisses.

Swirling questions overloaded her mind. Her nervous system seemed to collapse, and she fell back into the couch. Claire scratched Pip's back and belly, taking a few deep breaths.

Just breathe.

Claire pushed the unanswered questions out of her mind. She would deal with the aftermath tomorrow.

Her thoughts swung to the left. Seeing an image of Luke in her mind, her body and nerves immediately calmed. She took it in, reveled in it, and balanced her center. She would address the ramifications of the undeniable attraction later.

Bath.

Sleep.

Claire followed her plan. She ran a bath, undressed, and slipped into the heated water. She soaked, letting the water seep into her pores, praying the chill still clutching her would disappear. After an hour of trying, Claire relented and headed for bed. Wearing her warmest pajamas and socks, she slipped under the covers. Pip jumped on the bed, snuggling in against her. The feel of him was reassuring. Instinctively reaching for the lamp, she hesitated, then turned it off.

She blinked, finding herself once again at the bottom of the well, but there was no water. Crouching down, she clawed at the ground with her nails. The injured ground began to bleed. The area around her feet pooled with the thick crimson liquid. A claw erupted from beneath her feet, grasping her ankle. Claire screamed, struggling against the grip. The blood bubbled into the small area faster. A rush of water hit her legs, toppling her to the ground, soaking her in the icy water and blood. A second clawed hand broke through the surface, pulling her down, the water reaching her chin. There was no escape. She took a deep breath. The water overtook her height. The charred skull came into her sight, waiting for her. She opened her mouth in a terrorized scream, her mouth filling with the iron-tasting liquid.

Claire's eyes shot open, her lungs choking on a scream. Coughing, in a desperate attempt for air, she rolled. The contents of her mouth spilled onto the floor, a mixture of water and blood. Claire gasped, hyperventilating in sheer panic, her eyes tearing. Feeling the bed beneath her and Pip beside her, she reached for the light, almost knocking over the lamp. She searched the illuminated room for any shadows or signs of mischief. Her heart still thudded in her chest.

Pip turned with a jerk, jumping off the bed and staring into the darkness beyond the room. Claire's stomach filled with dread at the adjacent living area. All her instincts told her someone or something was hiding, waiting in the darkness, watching. In confirmation, Pip growled.

Her eyes fell on the clock, 3:36 AM.

She looked for her cell phone and remembered the well. The horrid face flashed in her mind's eye. Paralyzed by fear, she couldn't move. Her only action was to stare at the blackness just beyond the open door.

Screw this.

Claire jumped out of bed, slammed the door closed, then scurried back to the bed like a child. Her body shook. Her only act was to stare at the closed door and wait for daylight.

The first rays of the sun breached the drapes of the room. Claire scurried from the bed, opening the curtains. The sunlight dispelled whatever perceived menace had existed in the darkness. She opened the closed door. Pip trotted into the partially lit room without incident.

Releasing a long-held breath of relief, she sat on the edge of the bed, questioning her sanity. The deep cold still clung to her. While she wanted to shake the feeling of dread, it seemed impossible. Determined to cast the experience off, Claire donned her running clothes and shoes.

"Come on, Pip!"

A beat of hesitation made her pause before she moved through the once-threatening room. Reaching the main door, Pip at her heels, she couldn't help but turn back, surveying all the details of the room, her heart pounding. It all seemed perfectly normal. She yanked open the door with resolve.

Claire and Pip exited the hotel and began their jog. Claire had specifically chosen the hotel because of its convenient location to a running park only a block away. The fresh cold air and beautiful autumn scenery helped to clear her mind and invigorate her body despite the lack of sleep.

There were a few other joggers in the park. She appreciated the solace. Letting her mind wander but practicing walking meditation proved more difficult than usual. Too much had happened. Too many conflicts were slamming her conscious logical mind at once.

Could she have expected to be the producer of a paranormal ghost hunting show and never have an experience? Of course, she had. While *Finders* had found evidence numerous times, supporting the belief in paranormal activity, it was all more or less benign. Nothing dangerous or malicious, except for some scratches, which even then were limited to the dermal layer and disappeared almost immediately.

Why am I trying to rationalize any of this? There is no logical answer.

Hearing someone call her name, Claire stopped, midstride, scanning the area. Not seeing anyone, she restarted her pace. Out of the corner of her eye, a senior man jumped into her line of sight. Claire moved to avoid him. He yelled her name. She jerked in confusion. Looking around, she saw only Pip. He simply looked at her, patiently waiting.

Taking a breath, Claire bent forward, leaned against her legs, and closed her eyes.

Focus, Claire.

Dressed and out the door by 5:30 AM. Luke started his jog. Earbuds in, he stopped to stretch and then started his warmup. Jogging was his time to think. Any time there were too many conflicting thoughts or a puzzle to ponder, he went for a jog. Today was one of those mornings after the events of the previous few days, specifically last night. Finding Claire in the room with Kelsey James, the girl who'd tried to strangle her just hours before, was more than disturbing. What was worse was Luke knew the girl was not in control. There were other forces at play and, for whatever reason, they were focused on Claire. His body surged with heat. The unrelenting warmth cascading through him was foreign and yet seemed like home.

Crap.

Luke stopped, leaning against a tree. He stretched his calves, wishing for his mind to focus. His heart pounding, Luke pulled the earbuds out and took in the view. When Claire had kissed him before running for the helicopter, it stirred something deep. He had decided to shut down any feeling he had for Claire, for her good. There was no reason to follow a path they could never walk together.

The kiss made his plan impossible. Whether she knew it or not, Claire Westin was now a part of him, heart and soul. There would be no shutting her out or letting her go.

That was a problem.

If there was any morning in her life Claire needed her coffee fix it was that morning. She debated ordering two Venti Toffee-Nut Lattes right off the bat, skipping the whole debate that would come later.

Claire exited her car, taking in the warm sunshine and fresh air. She crossed the parking lot to the entrance of the coffee house, hearing a woman calling out in distress. Following the sound, she found an older woman who'd lost a few apples. Literally, a handful of apples had fallen from a torn bag. Claire moved to the woman's aid. "Let me help you with that."

"Thank you, dear," the elderly woman replied with a smile.

Claire gathered the dropped produce.

"I'm not sure how they got away?"

"I think your bag ripped," Claire said, handing the woman the fruit. "I can run inside and get another."

The woman adjusted the bag, putting the apples in her purse. "No, it's fine. My daughter is waiting for me right over there. Thank you for your help." She looked up, her eyes widening. "So beautiful."

Claire looked at her in confusion. "Excuse me?"

"Your light is so beautiful and bright. I haven't seen one like it in a long time. It's a beacon to be sure."

"My light?" Claire asked.

"Your spirit, of course," the woman replied, her eyes gentle and kind. "Your aura."

"You can see my spirit?"

"Oh, yes, I would have to be blind not to. I would take care to cover it up, or you'll have all of the lost souls looking for you."

"Wait. What?" Claire said, but the woman just smiled and walked ahead.

A younger woman, Claire assumed the daughter, met the woman in the parking lot. "Mom, you okay?"

"Yes, dear, I'm fine, just a little produce mishap," the elderly woman said. The pair resumed their journey to their car.

Claire stood silent until an annoyed consumer honked their horn. She blinked and walked into the coffeehouse. Completely dazed, she automatically ordered her coffee and left.

Claire sat in her car, rerunning the conversation through her mind, looking for an answer. Her spirit? Her aura?

Claire drove back to the hotel still dazed but determined to research what the woman had said. She'd heard of auras before, a colored halo surrounding a person. Spiritual Energy of some kind. Some believed some gifted people could see them. Was that what had just happened? Why was this the only time anyone had ever said anything to her, especially if what the woman said was true and she glowed? Edward Cullen popped into her mind. She giggled.

Polished wood, marble walls, brilliant stained glass, there was nothing as flamboyant or prolific as a Catholic Church. Rosary in hand, Luke knelt in a pew beside the confessional, his mind heavy with thoughts of his lost friend and the guilt surrounding the horrid image of Daniel's lifeless body hanging in the morning sun. In his last days, agitation and conflict had put a strain on their once-strong partnership. Luke found himself helplessly bereft about the loss of an innocent, Jenny

Ann. Daniel had insisted on focusing on the cryptic message the Demon spouted in Jenny Ann's last hours. Luke argued and pleaded for him to let it go. Daniel himself had driven the rules of demonology into Luke's life, the most crucial being to not put any credence into the rantings of a Demon. It was all a part of the manipulation. Listening, engaging, or giving in would be opening oneself to the Demon and the evil forces driving it.

Luke had arrived early that day for morning prayers. The gardening staff had discovered Daniel's body and were attempting to cut him down off the church steeple before anyone else could see. Unable to surmise how the man got out onto the angled roof to kill himself, they were forced to call the fire department and police for assistance.

There was no note, just a body.

Unable to shake his friend's dark decision, Luke stood in the middle of nowhere, on a ghost hunting team. He was thinking about the events of the past forty-eight hours in astonishment over God's ability to change one's life instantly.

Claire.

As a demonologist, it was imperative he remain pure in his faith and intentions so as not to give the unholy anything to grasp at when doing battle. Earthly ties, unchecked emotions, and passion for anything beyond his faith were dangerous to himself and those souls he fought to save.

His friends and family accepted his hermit lifestyle. They'd grown accustomed to his need for solitude and peace, but removing himself from the temptations of the current world had its difficulties. Keeping his life off the grid kept him safe. So far.

Claire.

He was desperate to touch her soft skin, kiss her perfect pink lips. The electricity of every touch, every look since he'd pulled her out of that stupid well remained a blazing pulse through his mind, body, and soul, driving him toward a place he'd left empty for years without thought or regret.

The confessional door opened and closed. Luke watched the red light turn green before opening the entrance to the booth. Stepping inside the darkened closet, he knelt at the window. "Bless me, father, for I have sinned. It's been two weeks since my last confession."

"What do you have to confess, my son?"

"I'm struggling with my feelings."

"In what way?"

"I'm having feelings for a woman."

"Is she married?"

"No."

"Are you married?"

"No, but I'm a man of faith in defense of the soul. My training strictly prohibits me from opening myself up to the temptations of the flesh."

"What about the temptations of the heart?"

"I don't see how they can be separated."

"While the guidance of your training is imperative, it is only guidance. You are a devout soldier of God and as such must question your motivations. Are you resisting this connection because of your training or out of fear? What exactly are you feeling?"

"Elation, calm, serenity, joy."

"Those are all voices of God. Why shut them out?"

"Because in them, I develop an attachment, a weakness in my faith."

"I don't hear weakness, my son. True, pure love is a gift from God and can only be used against you if you let it. Your faith in each other can be, and should be, as strong as your faith in God."

Exiting the confessional, Luke moved to the back of the church looking for the clergy office. Seeing an open wooden door, Luke knocked as he peered inside. An elderly priest was reading a book by the large window.

"Yes, come in."

Luke smiled and entered the room, "Hello, my name is Luke Melloy. I'm here investigating the recent incidents at Crestwater Church."

"Nice to meet you, Luke. Are you with the ghost hunting team they brought in to debunk the James girl's story?"

"Not necessarily to debunk. If what is thought to have happened there is true, there is a demonic problem in the church," Luke replied.

The priest's eyes narrowed into a familiar look of disapproval. "How can I help you?"

"I was wondering if the church archives have any additional information about Crestwater? Any information you may have would be appreciated."

"Very well, I'll take you to the archive."

The priest led Luke down the hallway to a secondary room. Unlocking the door, he opened it and led the way inside. The confined area was lined with dust-covered boxes, bookshelves, and file cabinets. It held a vast amount of information.

"Good luck. I think the earliest files are in the back left corner."

"Thanks."

Taking a seat in a wing-backed ivory chair, Claire smiled reassuringly at Reginald and Susan James. Situated in the living room of their lovely and comfortable home, Claire's Cameraman, Craig Brower, set up in preparation for the James interview.

"We have a few minutes before we get started," Claire said. "The interview will be a conversation, me asking you questions about you and your family, Kelsey's childhood, her friends, her relationships. If any topics seem too personal or upsetting, please let me know. Do you have any questions?"

"No, I think we're clear," Reginald James replied, adjusting his position in the love seat where he and his wife sat. With their hands linked, the body language spoke volumes. These two people were united, strong, and of the same mind.

"Before we begin, I wanted to say thank you for doing this," Susan James offered, squeezing her husband's hand. "We appreciate being able to tell our side of the story to set the record straight about Kelsey."

"Of course, we'll do our part in telling Kelsey's story."

The interview was insubstantial. Kelsey James was a good girl, best friend, cheerleader, and a social media darling. It was all the boyfriend's fault. The only reason Claire had agreed to the interview was because they'd allowed private access to the girl's bedroom.

"Thank you for taking the time to speak with us about Kelsey. Thank you for authorizing us to speak with Kelsey directly. We're looking forward to visiting with her later today," Claire offered, putting her notes away and picking up her bag.

"It was the least we could do after what happened," Mrs. James said her gaze dipping to the floor. "Were you still interested in seeing her room?"

"Oh, my goodness, yes. It completely slipped my mind," Claire said, looking to Craig.

Susan James smiled, rising from the couch. Claire followed her through the kitchen and down a hallway littered with family pictures. Kelsey was an only child. Claire eyed a door at the end of the hall, assuming it was Kelsey's room. They reached the room and stopped.

Claire waited patiently, watching the traumatized mother

stare at the door. Her eyes filled with fear and doubt.

"Mrs. James, are you—" Claire started, her guilt about the situation taking hold.

"I haven't changed anything in Kelsey's room. We're hoping the familiarity will help with her recovery," Susan said, pushing open the door, allowing Claire access.

Claire stepped into the teenager's sunlight filled room. Mirrors, mementos, band posters, collages of pictures, bulletin boards filled with random ripped magazine pages, quotes, and cat pictures covered the walls. At the head of the room, to Claire's back, stood a large fireplace littered with candles. The entire room was covered with candles, black, white, red, pink, and a few swirling.

The teenage space hit her subconscious as familiar, and she didn't know why. The clock inside her head started ticking. Claire scanned the details, working her way around the room. First, she used the panorama photo option on her phone, taking three separate photos. Next she made a quick list in a small notebook of pictures, makeup, clothing, shoes, amulets, incense, a stack of movies, a candle-making kit tucked into the back of the closet, and an unopened box of condoms hidden in the window seat.

"Whoa, someone liked candles," Craig said, stepping into the room. "Nice room."

"Yeah, it's lovely."

"You ready?"

"Yeah," Claire said, while stealthily placing one of the red and white swirled candles into her bag. "I think we're good."

Claire's body went cold, images flashing at blinding speed within her mind. She saw Kelsey surrounded by candles. A copper bowl was shining in the flame light. Kelsey said something inaudible before raising a knife and slicing at her forearm. The wound split blood into the copper bowl.

"Claire, are you okay?" Craig asked.

Returning to reality, Claire replied, "Yeah, I just got a little light-headed. Let's wrap up."

Claire followed Craig out of the room and down the hallway. Craig stopped saying goodbye to Mr. James.

"Did you get everything you needed?" Mrs. James asked Claire, her eyes red and puffy.

"Yes, I think we did. Thank you," Claire said and then hesitated. "I do have a quick question, if I may?"

"Of course, anything."

"Was Kelsey into the Occult or Witchcraft?"

"Of course not!" Mr. James exclaimed at the question.

"Why would you even think that?" Mrs. James asked.

"We saw a lot of candles and candle-making equipment in her bedroom," Claire replied the picture show from the bedroom still running through her mind. "I also noticed her bedroom is almost a replica of one in a recent occult movie out this summer."

"Having a hobby and liking scary movies do not make our daughter a devil worshipper!" Mr. James said.

"No, it doesn't. Using your blood in your candle making might," Claire replied, the words spilling out before she even had time to comprehend them. Without a thought, Claire moved to the door and made her exit. She could feel Craig shadowing her. She waited for him to settle into the truck, before saying, "I have no idea."

"What?"

"I have no idea where any of what I said to them just now came from," Claire said. "I just . . . I just knew. Something was feeding me information. Telling me what to say. I do know it is all true, though."

"How?"

"I saw it. I saw Kelsey do it."

"That's impossible, Claire."

"I know."

Three hours later, Luke pulled into the Sanitarium parking lot. Meeting Grant in the lobby, he signed them in at the desk and handed over their identification, telling the nurse they were there to see Kelsey James.

Directed to a secondary waiting room, they met Claire. She rose from her chair to greet them.

"Hey, Claire," Grant said, giving her a quick hug.

"Hey, Luke," Claire said with a bright smile, stepping forward and hugging him. The contact was brief, but Luke felt her stiffen in his embrace. She pulled back, her eyes distant and unfocused. He was about to ask her if everything was okay when a bearded doctor in a white lab-coat approached the group, "Ms. Westin?"

"I'm Claire Westin. You must be Doctor Rhue," Claire replied.

The doctor extended his hand, but Claire elegantly shirked it by introducing Grant and Luke. They both shook the doctor's hand while she asked, "Has there been any change in Kelsey's condition?"

"No, unfortunately, not, I'm not sure you are going to be able to get the information you are looking for."

"Are we still able to visit with her?" Grant asked.

"Yes, her family has cleared you to be able to try and interact with Kelsey. Maybe you'll be able to get a response." Doctor Rhue replied.

They followed Doctor Rhue down a long hallway and through a set of security doors.

"What is the initial diagnosis?" Grant asked.

"Paranoid schizophrenia as magnified by a traumatic delusional state," the doctor replied, leading them through the halls of the facility to stop at a locked room. Unlocking the door, he ushered them into an empty observation room.

"Is there a family history?" Luke asked. The small group took in Kelsey's weakened state via the glass between the rooms. The dark-haired beauty looked sick and frail. Kelsey's olive skin had paled as if from lack of sunlight. Dark circled under her eyes, and bruising showed on her exposed arms.

"None documented, but these disorders were many times mislabeled in the past, diagnosed with everything from laziness, attention deficit, retardation, to possession. Thankfully, recent days have put some clarification into the diagnosis, allowing us to help these people. The brain and its functions are still a widely unknown mystery."

"The trauma being whatever happened at Crestwater Church?" Luke asked.

"Yes," the doctor said. "I agreed to this session in the hopes your presence will bring her out of the current catatonic state."

"If her family has been unable to pull her out, why would you think a group of strangers would?" Claire asked.

"Strangers hold less of a threat than someone familiar," the doctor explained.

Flashes of Kelsey struggling to escape the church flooded Claire's mind. Where they were coming from, she didn't know. Were the images a figment of her imagination?

"We don't want to overwhelm her. You can interview her one at a time. As discussed, Mr. Henley will go first. Ms. Westin and Mr. Melloy can watch from here in the observation room. We'll be videotaping the entire session, and I'll be in attendance with Mr. Henley," the doctor said.

"Perfect, seems like we're all set," Grant said.

"Let's begin," Doctor Rhue said, motioning to Grant into the adjacent room.

Watching the doctor and Grant enter Kelsey's room, Claire

found herself overcome with a flash of heat, like standing too close to a blazing bonfire. She unconsciously took a few steps back.

Grant took a seat on one side of Kelsey. The doctor stood on the other. The doctor was talking to Grant about ways to try and wake the sleeping girl. Grant tried several different methods, taking her hand, calling her name, just talking to her. There was no response. Twenty minutes passed with little to no success. Claire and Luke stood silently, waiting.

"Do you think she can hear them?" Claire asked.

"Studies have shown patients benefit from their loved ones interacting with them despite their unconscious state."

"Is this different because she is catatonic and not comatose?"

"Possibly. Catatonic schizophrenia is a brain dysfunction, while coma is more of the body's way of shutting down to utilize all of the needed energy to repair itself," Luke explained. "The catatonic state may be Kelsey's brain trying to reconcile the trauma she endured at the church. Physical or metaphysical, one thing is for sure. Kelsey James will never be the same again."

"Metaphysical," Claire said, studying Luke's response. He wouldn't meet her eyes, and a small chill shook her. "You think something attacked Kelsey in the church? Perhaps the same thing that attacked me?"

"Yes," Luke replied with a low tone.

"Time to wake up, Kelsey," Claire murmured under her breath, turning away from the heartbreaking image. Despite her recent violence, Claire couldn't help but be concerned for the girl, even if she'd brought it upon herself.

"Claire," Luke said. Claire turned, seeing Kelsey's eyes open and the girl's face contorted. Nausea pooled at the back of Claire's throat. Her spine went rigid. Pain etched the back of her neck like a claw wrapping around her throat.

Luke and Claire watched Grant, and the doctor attempt to engage Kelsey. The teenage girl sat still, her gaze fixed on Claire.

"Claire, come here," Luke said motioning for Claire to join him on the other side of the room. "Slowly."

Claire complied. Luke watched the girls' eyes track Claire's movement like a hunter tracking its prey.

"Luke," Claire gasped, and Luke focused.

Claire's usually clear eyes were fogged. He took her hand and discovered she was cold to the touch, as cold as when he'd pulled her out of the well.

"Just focus on me," Luke said, squeezing her hand and knocking on the window between the rooms. A tingling sensation pulsed through Luke's body. Consciously pushing the energy to Claire, he drank in the experience while taking deep breaths. Claire's eyes cleared, and her hand warmed. "Better?"

She nodded. At the same moment, the door opened. Grant entered the small room, his eyes immediately focusing on their joined hands. "Is everything okay?"

"Yeah, I just got a little light-headed," Claire said, releasing Luke's hand.

Luke shot a look at Grant. "How did it go in there?"

"She opened her eyes, and we thought we were getting somewhere, but then we lost it. Not sure what happened."

"We might know," Luke said.

Claire shot him a deadly look.

Luke explained what happened in the observation room.

"Seriously?"

"Yeah."

"There's only one way to know for sure," Grant said, looking at Claire.

"What?" Claire asked.

"We need to test the theory," Luke replied.

"How?"

"By putting the stimulus back in the equation. First in the observation room, and then in the room with Kelsey," Grant said.

"You're not serious?" Claire replied, turning away from the men.

"Claire, if Kelsey is attracted to you for some reason, we have to investigate and see where it leads," Grant replied.

Claire ran her hands through her hair. She stood silent for a moment before turning and meeting Luke's eyes. She seemed to be searching for something. An acknowledgment or reassurance? He couldn't give anything to her and looked away.

"Claire, there's something you need to know," Grant said.

Luke's stomach dropped. Listening to Grant explain to Claire what had happened at the hospital when they found her in Kelsey's room made him physically ill. He kept his focus elsewhere, not wanting to watch Claire's reaction to the news. The incident was his fault. He should be able to protect her.

"Fine," Claire said. "Yeah, okay, let's see what happens."

Luke turned, seeing the determination in her eyes.

Grant returned to Kelsey's room and quietly informed the doctor Luke would be entering the room next, then stepped into the hallway and motioned to Luke. The two men switched places.

Luke stepped in, noting how cold the room felt compared to the hallway. "Hello, Kelsey, my name is Luke Melloy. I want to speak with you about Crestwater Church." The girl lay motionless. "Kelsey, can you hear me? We're here to help you, but you have to tell us what happened. We went to Crestwater. I gotta tell you, Kelsey, the church is a pretty creepy place. I would understand if you're hesitant about sharing your experiences." Luke took her hand. "Kelsey, you're safe here in the hospital. Surrounded by people who are here to help you through this trauma."

The door opened. Grant walked into the room, followed by Claire. Luke shook his head.

The doctor audibly sighed, "I want to thank you for trying. Your help is sincerely appreciated."

"It is our pleasure," Luke replied, watching Claire and Grant approach the bed.

Kelsey lay quietly, the shadows of her face dark and haunting despite the harsh hospital lights. Luke watched her closely while alternating his focus on Claire.

Nothing.

Silence.

Luke looked to Grant and then Claire. Claire exhaled a deep breath, the warmth of her breath mixing with a sudden iciness in the air. He switched his focus to Kelsey, whose eyes opened. Her skin tightened against the bones of her face. Her eyes stared out with a menacing black glare. The room filled with the stench of death and sulfur.

"Kelsey?" Luke said. A guttural, yelping laugh of malevolent spite and rage emanated from the thin girl's physical form. "Who are we speaking with, if not Kelsey?"

"He who is not him or her. He who will make the dripping climax of blood at your feet," the Demon within Kelsey replied, licking its lips while looking at Claire.

An unearthly scream filled the room. *Claire.* Her face ashen and eyes wide in terror, she stumbled back. Grant moved to catch her, and Luke re-focused.

"God and Father of our Lord Jesus Christ, I appeal to your holy name, humbly begging your kindness, that you may graciously grant me help against this unclean spirit now tormenting this creature of yours, through Christ our Lord."

"Save her, Luke. Save her as you did Daniel!" the Demon cried. The room shook, the lights flickering.

"I armor myself today with the power of the Most Holy Trinity, in the oneness of God, Creator of the universe. I armor myself today with the baptism of Christ, His crucifixion and resurrection, His ascension and glorious second coming."

"There is no hope for her light! It is already marked with the seed of Belial!"

"I armor myself today with God's guidance to direct me, God's might to sustain me, God's wisdom to instruct me, God's word to give me speech, God's shield to protect me, God's army to defend me, against the snares of demons, against the lure of vices, against all who plot me harm."

"Centum quinquaginta animas sedem formabis radicibus!" the Demon spat out with a low growl.

As quickly as the episode began, it ended. Luke checked the room. Claire stood shielded within Grant's protective arms, while the doctor huddled in the corner of the room.

Shit.

Claire, her mind on fire, ran from the room, away from the cold death encapsulating her thoughts, searching blindly for isolation, solace from the image now burnt in her memory. There was none. Only the gleaming of starch white walls, slick shining vinyl floors, and the smell of bleach. Dizzying nausea drained the warmth from her cheeks. She gulped back the bile pooling in her throat. Blindly entering a random door, she ran for the bathroom, then hurled the contents of her stomach into the toilet. Hysteria took over. Seeing the shower, she stepped inside and turned on the water, desperate to rid herself of the vile stench overwhelming her senses. Collapsing against the wall, she slid down, curling into a fetal position against the cool, smooth tile, the pounding water saturating her body.

With her mind sluggish and steeped in thick blackness, she prayed for the water to wash away the malicious images clawing at her mind. All the hatred and depravity of the world poured through her veins, consuming her body. Pain, madness, fear, and agony pounded at her soul, unrelenting and hungry. Struggling to remain in control, she gasped for air, sobbing.

Somewhere in the distance of her mind, someone called her name. Her eyes remained closed, her body weary from the pain. Freezing, she shivered, despite the heated water. Gentle arms lifted her against the wall. A tender, steady hand cupped her cheek. A cascade of warmth flooded her body. She opened her eyes. Luke sat beside her, on the floor of the shower, propping her against him. She stared up at him, the dimness of the room giving his chiseled features a softness she wasn't expecting. His eyes watched her patiently, their deep brown pools inviting and supportive. He cupped her cheek and kissed her forehead. She grasped his hand in desperate need. Tears mingled with the water falling down her cheeks. He wrapped himself around her, encircling her in his protective embrace. She sobbed against his chest, the water drenching them both.

Grant paced the hallway outside the patient room for almost an hour before the door opened. Luke stepped out in a pair of blue scrubs.

"How is Claire?"

"I think the worst is over for now. She'll be out in a minute," Luke replied.

After they'd found her, Grant alerted the medical staff to Claire's sudden *illness*. The hospital staff allowed them the space to attend to her uninterrupted. The doctor in attendance during the episode with Kelsey offered a couple sets of scrubs and any assistance he could, all the while fumbling his words and looking rather ill himself.

"Is she talking yet?"

"No, not yet," Luke said, his face stoic and pale.

Grant had seen his share of demonic activity, even possession, but what had just happened was beyond anything he could've expected. His guilt for putting Claire in the situation pulled at him.

"At least now we know what we're dealing with," Grant replied. "What was it, Kelsey — the Demon — said before it stopped? Was it Latin?"

"Yeah," Luke replied, rolling his shoulders and stretching his neck. "One hundred and fifty-seven souls will lie at the base of your throne."

"What the hell does that mean?" Grant asked

Luke shrugged. "Don't know yet, but I'm gonna find out," Luke said, determined fire in his eyes. "Claire shouldn't have been there."

"I know," Grant said, shaking his head. "I know."

"Has anything like this ever happened to her before?"

"What do you mean?"

"I know Claire is the producer of the show, but has she ever had any paranormal experiences before? Anything she's ever told you about?"

"No, not that I know of," Grant said, searching his memory. "Claire has always handled the business of the show, but she's never shown any interest in the paranormal or the investigating. Why?"

"Just curious," Luke replied, his mind spinning with possibilities. "I think we need to call Shaun."

"Shaun? Why?"

"Because whatever this connection is between Claire and the Demon, we need to get control of it now. Shaun is the only person I know who would be able to give us some insight as to what is going on and how to stop it."

For Claire, there were no words, only exhaustion.

Grant drove them back to the hotel, their personal cars left behind for retrieval later. Luke ushered Claire into the passenger's seat and took the back.

Part of her hated the small distance between them, wanting to cling to the security of his warmth. The other part felt so far removed from the world around her, she barely noticed the stream of lights and sounds passing outside the window. Her body begged for rest, slumber, yet her mind whirled and bucked in chaos.

Claire was vaguely aware of getting out of the truck and being escorted to her room. Pip immediately greeted Luke, who took residence on the couch. Claire silently crawled into bed, staring at the popcorn ceiling. Sleep meant closing her eyes. Not an option. Closing her eyes meant seeing everything again, letting it back in or acknowledging it was lurking, waiting for her just beyond the thin line of conscious thought.

She needed a distraction, something to think about other than the awful feeling of dread lying attached to her stomach. She padded into the small living area of her room. Luke sat in silence. Claire wondered if he was asleep.

"Hey," he said, casting his warm eyes over her suddenly shivering body.

"I didn't mean to wake you," she said, taking a seat on the couch next to him.

"You didn't," he replied. "I was meditating."

"Meditating?" she said, while he adjusted the throw blanket on the back of the couch around her. "Very new-age of you."

"Pretty old school," Luke said. "New age to those who have just discovered it."

"Touché."

"Can't sleep?"

"Not even close," she said. "Maybe I should try meditating."

"Maybe you should," he said.

Claire wanted to laugh, but the calmness of his presence after what they'd all experienced made her hesitate. "Do you think it would help?"

"Can't hurt."

"All right, tell me how, because whatever I'm doing isn't working."

"Close your eyes," he said with a smile.

"Unless it includes that," Claire said, rising from her seat, walking away from him.

"Closing your eyes? Why?"

"I just . . . I can't right now."

"Claire, has anything like this ever happened to you before?" Luke asked, leaning his elbows on his knees.

"Like what?" Claire said, trying to avoid the question she knew he was asking. She wasn't sure which was worse—a fear of being delusional, or the fear of it all being real. She pulled the blanket closer around her body. Still not warm enough

"Like what happened to you in the field that day with Pip," he said, making her blood turn cold.

Damnit, he remembered! "I told you, it was heatstroke," she said. "I was hallucinating from dehydration and heat exhaustion."

"Are you sure?"

"Yes! I'm sure." His questions flooded her chest with anger. "This was a bad idea. Maybe you should go."

"If you want me to, I will," Luke said, rising from the couch.

Panic overtook the anger, and she stumbled over her inner

contradiction, not knowing what to do.

"Do you want me to leave?"

Jesus, woman, make up your mind already!

"I saw it," she blurted out, a fever of doubt and fear over-taking her senses. "It was huge and ugly and horrible. I saw the Demon, and I saw Kelsey! I heard her screaming in agony. I could feel her pain. The horrifying torture it's putting her through."

"Claire . . ."

"It stared right at me, through me." She continued confess-ing every secret she had held onto in the space between them. "It poured all of its hate and evil into me like a disease. Cancer infecting every pore, strangling me with every breath I take. I don't want it! No, I don't want you to leave. I want you to make it stop. Get it out of me, please, Luke!"

With her plea, he reached for her, wrapping his arms around her in comfort.

"Make it stop. I want it to stop."

"We'll make it stop," Luke said, holding her tightly against him. "I promise I'll make it stop." They stood silent wrapped within the moment. "You need to rest."

Claire nodded, sniffling as Luke led her into the bedroom. He arranged the bedding before she sat down. She crawled in, feeling naked without his warmth. "Try and get some sleep."

Her heart lurched, causing her to sit up, "Luke." He turned, the low light reflecting off his eyes. "Will you stay?" Feeling like a child asking a parent to protect them from the monsters under her bed, Claire straightened her back. Prepared for his rejection, she held her breath.

"Yeah, of course.," he said, moving to the opposite side of the bed. He didn't move back the covers but lay on top of them, Claire assumed to keep things professional.

They lay in silence. Luke focused on his breathing and thought she'd fallen asleep. When she turned to face him, he opened his eyes, seeing her beautiful face just inches away. His heart raced, and he begged it to calm. The need to touch her scorched his body. He held back.

"Can you feel it?" Claire said, her voice barely audible.

The question threw him off. Everything about Claire threw him off. In a desperate attempt to remain in control of his colliding emotions, he responded. "Feel what?"

Her soft and yet piercing gaze studied him. He could almost hear her mind working as she stared through his mask, a mask, until then, no one knew existed. She shifted slowly, her hand rising from the bedding before gently lying against his cheek. "Feel this."

With her touch, his world rolled and surged. His energy aligned into a powerful rush of endorphins and strength. Closing his eyes, he savored the surge, like taking in pure oxygen after years of suffocation. "Yes."

"What . . ." she began, and he watched her take a breath of air. " . . . is it?"

Her sweet breath touched his chin. Her lips brushed against his in a hesitant kiss. The union sent sparks flying through to his chest. Luke claimed her mouth with a fiery need. Taking her into his arms and rolling her beneath him, he could feel her desire, feel the heat boiling in both of their bodies. She opened to him, her nails curling into the back of his neck, demanding his attention. He devoured her mouth in response.

Delicious.

Intoxicating.

Heaven.

"Claire," Luke said, forcing himself to pull back from the elation. His body groaned in response.

"I know," Claire said, breathless and panting. "I know we have to stop."

Luke met her eyes, seeing clarity and understanding he wasn't expecting. "I don't . . ."

"I understand, Luke," she said, her thumb stroking his cheek. "It's complicated, and things are complicated enough right now." He collapsed against her, breathing in her scent. "Your being here, holding me in your arms is enough for now."

CHAPTER SIX

L uke and Grant escorted Claire down to meet Shaun. The stuffy business conference room they'd sequestered had morphed into a relaxing open meditation space with running water, greenery, and candles. There were several comfortable chairs and a couch on the far edge of the area.

Standing six feet and seven inches, Shaun Levy looked more like a linebacker than a Reiki Master. The solid, balding man greeted them with a wide, plentiful smile. "Gentlemen and lady, welcome." Extending his had specifically to Claire. "I am Shaun."

Shaun Levy was the most gifted and grounded Physical Medium Luke knew. Grant and the *Finders* team had utilized his skills on numerous occasions when the presence of a negative entity needed exorcizing.

From everything Claire had told Luke thus far, Shaun would be the best person to get her through this awakening. Shaun would be able to teach her how to fight back and control whatever abilities she might have. It would be a quick crash course, but worth it. Luke also hoped he could convince Shaun to come with them to Crestwater Church.

"Thanks for taking time out of your schedule for us," Grant said as they all shook hands. "We're in a bind and appreciate it."

"It is not every day I get summoned via private jet to join you in an investigation. Who am I to deny such an invitation? I prepared us some tea." Shaun gestured to a table in the middle of the seating arrangement set with a tea service for six.

Claire sat next to Luke. Not knowing what to expect, she felt oddly comfortable in the surroundings. Filled with sunlight, and plants, the room exuded a natural warmth. Shaun handed her a cup of tea, and she thanked him. Once they all settled in, Shaun's attention rested on Luke, who briefly explained the situation. He left out most of the details, which Claire assumed was intentional.

"Are we ready to get started?" Shaun asked, looking at Claire.

"Ready for what?" she asked.

"Ready for me to tell you what I see," Shaun replied with a relaxed smile. "Don't worry. There is no pain involved. You won't even know."

"Ah!" Claire exclaimed, suddenly feeling an intense piercing pain behind her left eye, like an ice pick piercing her retina. Her teacup fell out of her hand and shattered on the floor, and they all jumped.

"Shaun?" Grant said.

"It's not me," he replied.

Claire attempted to open her eyes as the pain increased.

"Claire, I need you to relax," Shaun directed. "Take a deep breath. In and out. Picture something calming like the waves of the ocean or a field of wildflowers swaying in the breeze."

Claire complied, but the pain continued.

"Luke, take her hand."

Claire felt her hand in his, the stroking of his thumb. The contact enabled her to distance herself from the pain. It was still there but subsided into a faint pulse.

"Claire, can you open your eyes?"

Claire's eyes opened, and she looked around the room. Grant was cleaning up her mess. "God, I'm sorry!" Her cheeks flushed in embarrassment.

"Don't worry about it," Grant said with a smirk.

Claire looked to Shaun, who stared intently at her.

"What did you see?" Claire asked.

"Not much. That worries me," Shaun replied. "Tell me what's been happening."

Claire, Grant, and Luke recounted the tale thus far, adding in the details. Shaun listened intently, rubbing his bald head. "Your light is magnificent. It's like nothing I've ever seen before. Your aura is blinding."

"Translation?" Grant asked.

"It means I can't see anything. I cannot move past it. A mere brush of my energy caused Claire's — your — defenses to rise, not against me, but yourself. There's something buried deep inside you, Claire. Something powerful. Whoever put your defense in place is fiercely protecting your power, even from you."

"The power has always been there?" Luke asked.

"As far as I can tell. It's not something able to build itself in a few days or weeks," Shaun replied.

"I have no abilities. I'm not psychic in any way," Claire said. "Why is all of this happening now?"

"Question of the day. If I had to guess, I'd say what happened at the church was an accidental trigger. It's like when you blend a bunch of ingredients in a dish, and the taste is amazing. In this case, something was playing with you and accidentally opened Pandora's Box."

"I'm the box."

"Yep."

"Now that the box is open they — aka the deceased — are all curious about it. You're a magnet, and the entities are experimenting with you to see what happens, what they can make happen."

"How do I close the box?" Claire asked.

"I don't know if you can."

"There has to be something we can do," Grant said.

"We can try to camouflage it, bury it somewhat with some shielding and misdirection. At least until you can break through the barrier and get some answers."

"If that's our best option, let's do it," Claire said with a nod, dismissing the part about having an unknown Pandora's Box attached to her soul. She remembered the tale of Pandora's Box, and it did not end well for humanity or the universe. Dread climbed her back, but Luke's hand appeared on her shoulder, pushing it away.

"We will need a few hours to get you settled into the basics of Reiki and meditation, but I think we can do it."

"Perfect—while you're learning from Shaun, we'll check in with the sheriff and get ready for tonight's investigation," Grant added.

"Sounds like a plan," Luke said, looking at Claire.

Claire took a deep breath and nodded. She could do this.

The car ride to the church was fast. Luke got lost in his head, recounting again everything surrounding them. Kelsey, the church, Claire, and the Demon in the middle of all of it. While he had suspected Claire had gifts she'd either suppressed or was just unaware of, Shaun's revelation was a little unsettling. Someone had bound Claire, effectively creating a wall between her and her abilities. Why, and to what end? Had the Demon somehow unbound Claire, thus creating all the chaos, or was there something more sinister involved? He didn't like it, any of it.

"So, you and Claire?" Grant asked, breaking Luke out of his thoughts.

"What about Claire?"

"Something you want to tell me?"

"There is nothing to tell."

"Stop right there. Who exactly are you trying to bullshit?"

"All right, fine, I admit there's a connection." He'd known the conversation would come soon or later. He was hoping on later but understood the need for sooner.

"This is new."

"Embryonic."

"I meant new as in not your style. I've never known you to get personally involved with a client."

"Claire is not exactly a client, is she?"

"Close enough, and beside the point. In the years I've known you, I've never seen you scared. Last night, in Kelsey's room, you were terrified, and not of the Demon — of what was happening to Claire."

"I just admitted there's a connection," Luke said. "What do you want me to say? Yes, I care about Claire, okay?"

"Ironic. Do you love Claire?" Grant asked.

Luke felt all the color drain from his face. "How can I even answer that?"

"You answer it if you know the answer. I think you do."

"I barely know her," Luke objected.

"Doesn't mean anything, and you know it," Grant replied. "Look, all I know is in the ten years I've known you, I've never seen or known of any woman to make you turn sideways or blink. Your purpose in life has always been obvious and focused. From what I can see, that is not the case any longer."

"Maybe it is," Luke conceded. "Regardless, my focus needs to remain on resolving our current challenge. Once this is over, I'll ponder any matters of the heart."

They pulled up to the church, not expecting the chaos they found. Dozens of tents were set up with even more people running around in medical garb. "What the hell is going on?"

Claire sat cross-legged on the floor, facing Shaun. A colored mat sat between her and the polished wood. She straightened her back to focus.

"The word Reiki is made of two Japanese words. Rei, which means God's Wisdom or the Higher Power and Ki, which is life force energy," Shaun explained in his soft, gentle voice.

She was still amazed at the gentle giant before her, her teacher and mentor.

Having to learn a whole new skill, master an entirely new set of senses in a few hours seemed impossible to Claire, but Shaun had already guided her through deep meditation and sensory awareness. Both had put her in touch with her newly developed senses, allowing her to control the intensity of each.

Claire learned a physical medium had as much, if not more, control over the activities directed at or around them. Spirits, entities, and other forms in the astral plane utilized her energy to feed their own needs. By controlling the strength of the energy she emitted, she could then control who or what used the power to communicate with her.

"Reiki is actually a spiritually guided life force energy.'"

"Reiki is utilized how?" she asked.

"When you encounter a spirit or open yourself to the spirit world, you are expending your life energy. If not recouped, this loss will take years off your life, causing illness, headaches, irritability, etc. Mastering Reiki will enable you to replenish any life force you lose, minimizing the damage to your Temple.

"Temple?"

"I called it a temple because it is not necessarily your body but the area around your body. Like a temple, you are always standing within."

"Got it," Claire said.

"One of the unique pieces of Reiki is it cannot just be developed and learned, but given, like a plant or a seedling given as a gift. Once it's accepted, it is up to you to nourish, tend, and grow the seedling into a plant. It takes time and dedication, but the rewards, as I explained, are numerous."

"You are going to give me the Reiki seedling?"

"Yes."

"Can I name it?" Claire asked in jest.

Shaun smiled. "If you were to name it, what would the name be?"

Claire scoured her mind for a suitable name for the seedling she was about to receive. What was a good name to accompany Pip? They would be siblings, after all. A name popped into her head, and her eyes lifted. All the breath in her body disappeared, and the blood from her face drained into her stomach.

"What's wrong?" Shaun asked in alarm.

Claire attempted to speak but could not find the words. The skeletal faced Demon stood staring just behind Shaun.

"Whatever you are seeing, Claire, push it out. Don't be afraid of it. You control the energy, Claire. Push it away."

Claire mentally gathered her strength, using the techniques Shaun just taught her, but the entity remained.

"Push it away, Claire. Face it and show it you're not afraid."

"I can't," Claire stuttered, her body quaking in fear. "Too strong."

The Demon, gruesome and disfigured, stepped closer to Shaun. Claire jumped to her feet. "Shaun look out!"

Before he had a chance to react, the Demon tossed him across the room like a ragdoll. Shaun hit the wall hard, crumbling to the ground, unconscious. "Shaun, no!"

Claire moved to assist her friend but was yanked back. The cold sting of metal scraped her neck, biting into her skin and squeezing. She was lifted off her feet and the metal tightened, quickly cutting off her air. She tried in vain to free herself, but the result was only more pain.

"Claire!"

A faint voice gave her a glimmer of hope as she choked, gasping for air. The metal noose tightened, piercing her skin. Her eyes watered, her limbs lost feeling. The blackness of death edged her vision.

No, not yet!

Claire used the skills she'd learned to pool her energy into her base chakra. It electrified her, the jolt of electricity shooting through her spine. Claire screamed aloud. Her mind was rebelling against the shock.

"Claire, hold on!" the voice broke through the chaos.

She focused, directed her energies. Her body landed hard. All the air pushed from her lungs left her choking and gasping for oxygen.

"Claire, are you okay?" Craig said, kneeling next to her on the floor.

"Shaun?" she managed to choke out.

It took Luke and Grant half an hour to find Sheriff Mingus amidst the chaos surrounding the church. When they did, he looked haggard and overwhelmed.

"Gentlemen, how can I help you?"

"What's going on?" Grant said.

"Chaos has come to Crestwater, thanks to you."

"Excuse me?" Luke said.

"It's not your fault. I guess the dead never really stay buried." He shook his head. "Your findings in the river the other day? They have multiplied exponentially."

"How so?"

"The team from Washington has found over one hundred sets of bones so far." He motioned to all the tents. "They are dating them and getting an official count, but it looks like most of them are between a hundred to a hundred and twenty-five years old. That's not even the worst part."

"It gets worse?"

"Yeah, a majority of the bones are either female or children under the age of ten."

"Shaun is okay. You're both okay," Craig said, helping Claire to the couch.

Her entire body shook. Pip jumped on the couch next to her. "I don't know if I can do this," Claire said her voice cracking and shaking.

"Claire, it's over. You and Shaun are fine."

"Shaun is not fine!" she protested, jumping to her feet. "This is all my fault!" Claire paced the small area.

"You stopped the attack," Craig said, helping a newly conscious Shaun to the chair. "I simply witnessed it."

"How can that be possible when I don't even know what happened?"

"Claire, listen to me," Shaun said, getting her attention. "You have powerful reactive defenses working at the mere whisper of a threat to you. Now you're starting to tap into your abilities. Your experiences and your defenses will only grow stronger. You may not know how you did it yet, but it was all you. You saved us both."

"I don't want it, any of it."

"Claire—" Shaun stepped toward her to console her fears.

"No, Shaun," Claire said sternly. "I'm done with all of it. Pippy, come!"

Claire turned her back on them, storming out the door with Pip.

Adrenaline and anger fueled her stride. Not knowing where she was going or even giving a second thought to caring, Claire walked. Her consciousness spun, questions, answers, random thoughts, and fears bubbling from the back of her mind. What was she thinking? She was a television producer, not Amy Allen. Her life consisted of ratings, marketing, and the bottom line. Nothing more. She didn't need Pandora's Box, nor did she want this gift. Not a gift — a tragedy, a hindrance, a complication, not a blessing. Not from where she stood. On cue, a screaming woman appeared in front of her on the street.

"Not now, please leave me alone!" Claire said, stepping to the side, forcing her mind to focus and build the walls Shaun just taught her how to build.

She walked in the direction of the park. Fresh air would do her good. Twenty minutes later, she heard Grant's voice calling her name. She released a small sigh of relief. It wasn't Luke. She wasn't sure she could think straight right now. Luke's apparent juju over her wasn't going to help clear her head.

Grant stopped beside her, pulling her into a hug. "Hey, are you okay?"

"I think I'm losing it," she said in her calmest voice, the panic welling in her stomach like a bubble about to burst. "I'm not a psychic or a medium. I'm a television producer. I make good television. I film people who are losing their minds. It's entertaining. I'm not one of those people."

"No, no, you're not," Grant said in a reassuring tone, calming her nerves. "You're Claire Westin, daughter of billionaire Albert Westin. You're stubborn, successful, demanding, and amazing."

"I don't feel like her anymore," she protested, tugging on her ponytail in frustration. "I feel like I'm going crazy."

"I know you do," Grant agreed. "A lot has happened. It's difficult to take it all in, but you're handling it like a champ, which goes to prove my point. You're still Claire Westin. You've just gained a few more skills to add to the resume."

"You make it sound like I learned how to do a macro in a spreadsheet or some new editing technique. Waking up a physical medium is a little different, Grant."

"Yes, you're right. I'm not trying to minimize any of this, but I'm at a loss here. The woman I know and respect does not run from a fight. Yet here I am in the middle of Wyoming chasing you down the street. I'm a little out of my depth. I was half-tempted to send Luke, but I didn't want you two making out in a corner or something."

Claire's jaw dropped the blood rose to her cheeks, but she also found herself smiling. "There is nothing—"

"Nothing is going on between you and Luke. Oh, please. You're talking to *me*, Claire. It's written all over your face," Grant chided, seeming to concentrate on the change in subject.

"There isn't."

"The response is *there isn't anything going on yet,*" Grant replied. "It's fine. Whatever. I want you to be happy."

"Well, thanks, but he is the least of my worries at this point," Claire replied with a sigh. "How do people do this?"

"I haven't the foggiest, but I do know Shaun is an expert. He can help teach you, if you let him. Will you please come back? I know you can do this. You can handle this. Even if you can't, Melloy and I will be there to catch you if you fall."

"Melloy?"

"Yeah, Melloy, it's his name."

"His name is Luke," she replied.

"It's a guy thing," Grant replied. "We good?"

"Yeah, we're good," Claire replied. "One question though, how did you—"

"I'm a little psychic as well."

Grant and Claire regrouped with Craig, Luke, and Shaun.

Grant relayed the information the sheriff had given them to everyone's horror.

"Luke, you did some research at the local parish. Did you turn up anything?" Grant asked.

"Nothing. The parish records are all within the past fifty years. There was nothing about the church or past congregation."

"I might be able to help," Craig said. "In researching tonight's investigation, it seems all of the artifacts and documents from the Crestwater Church were put into storage about thirty years ago."

"Where?" Grant asked.

"The library. Some seem to think the artifacts have something to do with the disturbances. They didn't have any known incidents before the artifacts arrived."

"Perfect, two birds, one stone," Grant said.

"I'm going with you," Claire said from the back of the room.

"I'm going as well. Claire and I can weed through the historical data while you do the investigation," Shaun said.

"Sounds like a plan. It's just after three. Let's get something to eat and head out," Grant said to the group.

CHAPTER SEVEN

L ight flooded the storage room as the door swished open, dust billowing and filling the air.

School desks, chairs, and various furniture pieces were randomly stacked floor to ceiling throughout the area in front of them. To the right were rows of bookshelves filled with stacks of newspaper, cardboard boxes, and random items like lamps and printers.

"Good Lord," Shaun murmured under his breath. "Do we have any idea what we are looking for?"

"Nope," Claire replied with a small grin. She lived for research and found it especially fun when she had to dig for it. The history contained in the room was astounding. She guessed each forgotten item had a story to tell, stories trapped in the locked room for what she imagined were decades. Claire searched the walls for a light switch.

"Here," Shaun said.

She turned, seeing a pair of medical gloves in his hand. "Afraid of a little dust, Shaun?" Claire asked, flipping on the overhead lights.

"These are not for the dust. These are for the memories covered in dust."

"Explain, please."

"To a clairvoyant, physical touch is many times a contact point for visions. There is a lot of stuff in here with a lot of history. Unless you want a bombardment of visions over the next few hours, wear them."

"Understood," Claire took the gloves with a nod, pulling

them over her hands.

"Where do you want to start?" Shaun said.

"You go left. I'll go right."

"Sounds like a plan."

Luke signed into the visitor's log at the front desk of the Sanitarium. He'd had a side conversation with Grant, opting to forgo the investigation at the library in the hope he could ascertain Kelsey's condition. It was clear from their previous meetings some kind of demonic entity was present, but all of the encounters thus far had been provoked by Claire's presence. The Demon could be merely using Kelsey as a conduit to communicate. If that were the case, it would take a different means to remove the link than if the Demon had fully possessed Kelsey.

The Sanitarium seemed secure enough. Plexiglass windows worked as a barrier between the nursing staff and the waiting room. Every door needed key card access. The support staff, for the most part, seemed meaty and robust. None of these characteristics would have any effect if the Demon decided it wanted out, but it would delay any attempts if needed.

The door buzzed. The nurse announced Dr. Meddleshon was ready to see him.

New doctor?

Luke stepped beyond the barrier into the familiar sterile hallway. A robust gentleman greeted him in a lab-coat and suit.

"Luke Melloy?" the man asked.

"Yes, I was expecting to speak with Dr. Rhue. Is he not available?" Luke asked, the image of the doctor cowering in the corner of Kelsey's room after their last visit coming to mind.

"Unfortunately, no. Doctor Rhue has taken a leave of

absence. I'm handling Kelsey James' case now," the man said, offering his hand. "Jeff Meddleshon."

"Nice to meet you," Luke replied, shaking the man's hand with a firm grip.

"I have been reviewing the notes and tapes from your visit as well as Kelsey's overall care," Meddleshon said. "I have to say I'm at a loss as to what is happening with this poor child. I've also done some research on you, Luke. Your reputation precedes you. I'm sincerely looking for your assistance in helping Kelsey."

"That's why I'm here."

Two hours of shifting and sorting left Shaun and Claire with little more than they'd had when they started. A few articles about the church, which has been burnt down and rebuilt three times, added nothing as far as records from the original church or congregation. Claire wasn't giving up hope. There was still a lot to go through. Needing a break, she took a seat on a table, watching Shaun shift through a box.

"What's up?" he asked.

"Just taking a breather," she said.

"Good luck with that." Shaun laughed. "Try not to choke on all the dust."

"Yeah, really," Claire said. "I have a question."

"Shoot."

"Are there any advantages to being a medium?"

"Are you asking if the good outweighs the bad?"

"Yeah, I guess I am. Right now, all I'm seeing is bad. Is there a light at the end of the tunnel?"

"I've been a physical medium for most of my life. My grandfather was also a physical medium. He taught and nurtured me and my gift from an early age."

"It cracks me up. You call it a gift."

"It is a gift, Claire," Shaun said. "Look, I know you don't see it right now, but take it from someone who knows, it is a gift."

"Tell me how — why you think it is a gift?"

"I'm able to help the helpless. I'm able to give relief to the tortured and suffering. My — our — abilities allow for clarity and a view of life very few people will ever understand or get to experience. Yes, there is pain and darkness, but there is also light and joy. I'll never forget the first birthday party I went to after the emergence of my abilities. I could see joy and innocence. They are as tangible to me as a piece of paper in my hand. The knowledge of such beauty is beyond incredible. It gives me hope. Faith in the human spirit."

"Wow. I can't wait to experience even a little bit of what you described," Claire said, deeply touched.

"Oh, wait until you have your first orgasm. Talk about fireworks!" Shaun said.

Claire laughed aloud.

"You think I'm joking, but seriously. The spiritual beauty of two physical bodies in the throes of pleasure is awe-inspiring, and that is just sex. Making love to someone takes on a whole new meaning. It is the touching of souls. Completely spectacular."

Claire blushed.

"Plus, there is the bonus of being categorized as a superhero."

"Oh, my God, you've got to be kidding!"

"Come on! No medium besides me will ever admit it, but I'm an honest to God superhero with superpowers. How many people can say that?"

"Not many," Claire said between giggles.

"Damn straight," Shun said. "I'm going to get some water. You want some?"

"Yes, please," Claire said, wiping her brow before readying

herself to move another stack of boxes.

"Be right back."

"Thanks!" Claire took a breath, lifted herself off the table, and got back to work. She shifted the stack of boxes she'd left to the right into a space she'd created. There was very little space, so every inch helped. She moved one of the boxes. Some files slipped off the top tumbling to the floor.

"Crap."

Getting down on her knees, she scooped up the various pieces of paper and folders. A couple of the sheets slipped beneath the shelves. She reached beneath to recover them. Glancing beneath the space between the floor and the bottom shelf, she eyed a shadow and a glint of metal.

While stacking and reorganizing the fallen documents, her mind wandered back to the glint of metal. Curious, she left the remaining papers, seeing nothing of interest amongst them, and decided to see if she could weave her way back to the location of the glimmering object.

Shifting more boxes and furniture, she slowly made her way into the corner. A final set of bookshelves were all that stood in her way. She unloaded the shelves closest to her destination, shifting them against the others. Shadows darkened the small area. She used the flashlight on her phone to illuminate the corner.

Bingo.

Luke found Dr. Meddleshon very informed and open to everything Luke offered, a refreshing relief to the typical psychiatric rhetoric he was used to encountering. They developed a plan for how to monitor and engage Kelsey.

Entering Kelsey's well-lit room a few hours later, he was prepared for anything. Whether he would be speaking with Kelsey or the Demon would remain to be seen. He hoped to meet Kelsey. He wanted to get to know the girl, understand her point of view, and whether she was at all aware of what was happening to or through her.

She'd been heavily sedated since their last visit, but the doctor had given her a drug cocktail about an hour before to make her lucid for their talk.

When he walked into the room. Kelsey's eyes, clear and blue, immediately focused on him.

"Hi, Kelsey, how are you feeling today?"

"Sleepy, but okay I guess," she replied. Her skin, while pale, was a normal tone. Her body seemed unscarred or bruised.

"My name is Luke Melloy. We've met once before. Do you remember me?" Luke asked.

She studied him, apparently carefully searching her mind, but then responded by shaking her head. "Sorry, I don't remember much these days. Are you a doctor?"

"No, I'm not. I'm a teacher."

"Is this about the school? I know I've missed a lot, but I promise I'll make up all of the work as soon as I can."

"Not that kind of teacher," he said, smiling at her. "I'm sure the school will understand the situation and do everything they can to support you."

"Oh," her young face scrunched. "What kind of teacher are you?"

"I'm a theology teacher at a school far from here."

"What are you doing here, then?" she asked, idly playing with the strands of her long dark hair. "I don't believe in God."

"First off, I'm impressed you know what theology is, and second, is there a reason you don't believe in God?"

"It just seems like a fairy tale to me," she said, her teenage attitude showing. "Like something someone made up to brainwash people into giving them money and follow the rules, ya know? No offense."

"No offense taken."

"It's all a big business, if you ask me. The church says the money is going to support the poor and the hungry, but you know it's not. It's just going to the church bank account. Funding their great cathedrals with all of the marble, gold, and shit."

"I don't disagree." *I like this girl.*

"If you're here to make me see the light or some stupid shit, you're wasting your time. I'm good."

"I'm not here to do anything but talk," Luke replied. "I believe faith is very personal. I'd never try to convince you of anything you didn't want to learn about on your own. We've established you don't believe in God. Are you spiritual?"

"I guess you can say I am," Kelsey said, still absorbed in the strands of her hair. "I'm more into magic and nature."

"Wicca?" Luke said.

Her attention focused back on him.

"I'm a big supporter of Wicca and its beliefs. The idea nature is a living breathing entity in itself is very interesting and encouraging."

"Yeah, except we are trying to kill it every chance we get."

"Yes, we are, but this is the way of the current world," Luke said. "You said you are into magic—have you ever dabbled in Wiccan spellcasting?"

"Like what?"

"Like using an attraction charm to connect with someone seemingly unattainable, or even a curse charm to punish someone who pissed you off?" Luke said.

Kelsey's eyes widened.

"Kelsey, everything we say here is confidential. Anything you tell me will not leave this room."

She pondered the statement for a moment, resuming her preoccupation with her hair before folding her hands in her lap, then met Luke's gaze again. "Yeah, I've messed around a little. Do you think the spells have something to do with why I'm here?"

"I'm not sure," Luke said. "Can you tell me about the night you went to the church with your boyfriend?"

Claire shimmied her way into the corner, eyeing the wooden chest. It reminded her of a hope chest she'd seen a million times at antique stores. The glint of metal was the reinforced metal attached to the bottom corners. Reaching for the leather grip on the side, she tugged. It barely moved. The sucker was heavy, wedged between the wall and the bookshelf. She would either have to try to drag it out into an open area or move the bookshelf. She debated the two options, deciding the bookshelf was the more accessible course of action. Moving out of the corner, Claire grabbed the end of the large wooden bookshelf and pulled. It moved easily. She pulled enough to get behind. Then she pushed, making enough room to turn the chest away from the wall.

Kneeling in front of the chest, she used her flashlight to examine it top to bottom. It seemed to be made of an oak or cherry wood and in remarkably good condition, considering its assumed age.

Should she wait to open it until Shaun came back?

Deciding to make sure this was the gold mine they had been searching for and not someone's hope chest, she moved to lift the lid. It wouldn't budge. Looking at the front again, she realized it was locked. The empty keyhole seemed to be mocking her.

Ugh . . . wait!

She pulled out her keys, recalling the odd old key she'd found in the church when looking for Pip. She'd found it in her jeans when they'd returned to the hotel and attached it to her keychain as a reminder of the ordeal.

Claire put the key in the lock. It fit perfectly. She turned it. *Click.*

Kelsey detailed for Luke the events of the evening, admitting not only had they participated in a séance, but she also had gaps in her memory. She didn't remember her boyfriend taking her home or how she returned to the church.

"What happened during the séance?"

"Nothing."

"Nothing?"

"It didn't work. I must've done something wrong, because we didn't connect with anything. We waited for a while and explored, but nothing happened."

"What was the last thing you do remember?" Luke asked.

Kelsey's forehead scrunched in thought. "I remember going into the back of the church. There was an old desk. Matt thought it would be cool to have sex on the desk, so we did. I remember getting dressed. I was pretty high at the time."

"You were high on marijuana?"

"Yeah, we like to smoke when we do séances. It opens the mind to allow the spirits to more easily connect with you," Kelsey said. "Next thing I knew, I woke up in the hospital. My mom was freaking out. My dad was pissed."

"What about the other night—do you remember leaving the hospital and going back to the church again?"

Her face went ashen. "No."

Luke remained steady and calm, giving her a reassuring smile.

"You have no memory of me visiting you at the hospital or here?"

"No," she said, staring down at her hands.

Luke gave her a moment to process his words. Her parents hadn't shared with her any of the events to protect her fragile state.

"What about a woman named Claire? Do you have any memory of meeting or interacting with her?"

"I'm bored."

"I'm sorry, Kelsey. You must be feeling overwhelmed," Luke said, reaching out to grasp her hand. It was cold.

"I'm not overwhelmed. I'm bored," Kelsey said, her voice thicker and raspy. Kelsey slowly faced him. Her eyes had gone from crystal blue to black, her skin a pale burnt yellow. "With you."

The click of the lock sent a chill racing up Claire's spine. She reached for the sides of the chest lid, lifting it with ease. Propping her phone against the cover of the open chest, she took in the contents. Papers, church relics, woven cloth, and books.

Jackpot

Claire dove in, carefully handling each item and examining it before placing it on the floor next to her hip. It was all priceless to anyone looking for a window back in time. The script was flourished and precise. She found a leather-bound book she thought might be a journal of some sort and placed it in her lap. Something shifted behind her, making an audible scrape against the floor. "Shaun?"

She waited, but there was no response.

Probably mice. She'd seen a few of them scurrying about while shifting furniture. As she reached back into the chest, something stabbed at her hand. She pulled back in pain. "Ow!"

Ripping off the glove, she grabbed her phone and examined her hand. Whatever it was had pierced the glove, leaving a cut in the center of her palm. "Son of a bitch."

Searching for the cause of her injury, she uncovered a massive ledger in the bottom of the box. Reaching for it with her gloved hand, she lifted it out. She heard the clang of metal within the box and saw a jeweled handle. She grabbed onto the handle with her ungloved hand. A bolt of electricity shot through her body. The pain was unbelievably intense, and she screamed.

Grant Henley finished his descent down the large center staircase of the Crestwater Library. He had completed his portion of the investigation. The library, built shortly after the town's foundation in 1803, featured two levels filled with stacks upon stacks of books. Impressive, considering the small size of the community. The owner had complained of moving books, whispers, and the sound of running amongst the stacks after business hours. On Grant's walk, with teammate Kate, they'd experienced several odd occurrences and hopefully caught them on film. The moving books were the one he wanted to debunk, thinking it was more of a kid's prank than the others. The librarian would come in and find books stacked in the space between the shelves as well as whole sections taken out and replaced in reverse order.

Grant looked up at the sound of his name to see Shaun walking toward him.

"Hey, how's it going in the dumping ground?" he asked, having examined the room briefly when Claire and Shaun started their search.

"Slowly," Shaun said. "Hey, have you seen Claire?"

"Ah, no but I've been walking around. What's up?"

"I'm not sure," Shaun said. "I went to get some water. When I came back, she was gone."

"You sure you didn't just miss her in the sea of junk?"

"I don't think so, I called out her name a few times, and she didn't answer," Shaun replied. "I checked the bathrooms. There's no sign of her."

"We have this place wired — let's go check the cameras." They headed to the main library desk where all of the monitoring equipment was set up. "Craig, have you seen Claire lately?"

"No, I thought she was in the dungeon with Shaun."

"Can you check the feeds? She seems to have wandered off."

"Sure."

Luke took a moment, grasping what'd just happened. The Demon had decided he was done talking to Kelsey. "Who are you? What do you want?"

"Questions, always with the questions you already know the answers to."

"Why are you here?"

"I wanted to chat. This seemed easier than visiting your dreams. They are so tortured lately what with the recent death of your friend."

"I will not engage with you. Leave Kelsey James' body now. *Oratio ad Sanctum Michaelem Archangelum. In nomine onspec Patris, et Filii, et in Spiritu sancto. Amen.*"

The Demon threw Kelsey's head back into the pillow, laughing.

"*Princeps gloriosissime caelestis exercitus, Sancte Michael Archangele, da nobis aciem adversus principes potestates principes autem adversus mundi rectores tenebrarum harum, contra spiritualia nequitiae, in caelestibus,*" Luke said, rising from his seat beside the bed.

"You fool," the Demon said. "If I wanted Kelsey James, I'd have her already. She invited me in! I've feasted on thousands. I do not need her unremarkable soul."

"All souls are of value to the demonic void, collecting innocent souls for war against the heavens."

"I've earned my place at the Master's side. My minions collect all I need. I have a new, greater task, a task to end you and all like you."

"Veni in auxilium hominum, quos Deus creavit ad eius est Instar et magnus apud quos redemit de tyrannide pretiumm diabolic onspect. Te martyrum candidatus Laudat onspe exercitus sui custos, et quod ecclesia Sancti protector; tibi tradidit Dominus animas redemptorum in redemptionis Dominus duci in coelum."

Kelsey's body thrashed. The Demon growled. Luke took the opportunity to grasp and uncork the bottle of holy water in his pocket, then splashed it over Kelsey's writhing body.

The fog, pain, and panic lifted. Claire found herself standing in the middle of a church, not in the library. It looked somewhat familiar but still foreign. The pews were filled with people. Their clothing was dated, early century, she guessed. A wiry thin man's voice boomed at the front of the church. Whimpering and cries of pain echoing behind him.

Claire moved forward, taking in the scene. Drawing closer, she saw a man and two young children standing to the left of the altar. They looked sullen and distraught. The children sniffled, tears running down their faces.

"As has been done before and we will do again in the name of our Holy Father. As His church, we will purge the evil from amongst us," the man bellowed. "With this fire, we will cleanse this poor woman's soul of evil, granting her safety of forgiveness in the gates of Heaven."

Claire reached the steps of the altar. Taking one at a time, she reached the final level as the priest looked up at the crowd.

"In this, we pray to the Lord for strength and protection in His eternal light. Amen."

The congregation responded. "Amen."

The priest moved away from the center of the pulpit, revealing the altar behind him. Stacks of wood and kindling were piled high on the altar, a nest of sorts. At the top was a woman, bound to the alter amongst the timber. The priest nodded to the altar boys standing in wait. Each boy proceeded to obtain a torch from behind the altar and present it to the priest. He blessed each torch and bowed in reverence. Once he'd finished, the boys lit the torches and walked to the altar.

"No!" Claire screamed.

No one could hear her. She ran toward the altar as it burst into flames. The heat of fire made her stumble back. She watched in horror as the woman was burnt alive.

Craig, Grant, and Shaun searched the footage but saw no sign of Claire exiting the storage room or walking around the library.

"Are you sure she isn't in there?" Craig asked.

"Let's check again," Grant said. "Craig, have all of the teams check in."

Grant and Shaun hurried to the other side of the building. Halfway there they stopped.

"Do you smell that?" Grant asked. "Is that smoke?"

The two men raced to the storage room. Black smoke pushed from beneath the partially sealed door.

"Craig, call all teams. Red alert, get everyone out. The library is on fire!" Grant shouted over the walkie-talkie.

Shaun reached the door first and turned the knob. He yelped, jumping back. The smell of burnt flesh mixed with the smoke. "Fuck!"

Grant removed his sweatshirt, wrapping around his hand before trying the door. It wouldn't budge.

"Claire!"

"Deus pacis conterat Satanam sub rogate ergo pedibus, captivos tenere homines non ut facias Ecclesia. Offer nostras preces in conspectus Altissimi, ut sine misericordia sumant super nos

Apprehendam draconem serpentem antiquum qui est Diabolus et satanas, et ligátum mittas in abyssum proiecit Ut nemo se seducat amplius gentes. Sed exorcismus!" Luke said.

The Demon continued to thrash and growl.

"If you do not need Kelsey James, then leave! Stop this foolish game of power. You will lose!"

"He shall come and mark her with the sight of Heaven and Hell. His flesh to her flesh, she will be enslaved to only he upon the will of the father of darkened light. She will be water and air. You will suffocate and shrivel, drown and fall from your grace in her name. The darkness will claim your soul," the Demon howled.

Luke froze, jolted in shock.

"Save me, please!" a child's voice cried, a sweet voice from Luke's past. "You said you would save me. Now I burn! I burn!"

"In the Name of Jesus Christ, our God and Lord, strengthened by the intercession of the Immaculate Virgin Mary, Mother of God, of Blessed Michael the Archangel, of the Blessed Apostles Peter and Paul and all the Saints, and powerful in the holy authority of our ministry, we confidently undertake to repulse the attacks and deceits of the devil."

With a final upward thrust, Kelsey's body relaxed into the bed, silent. Luke waited a moment before he moved to check her coloring and vitals. Back to normal. Falling into the chair behind him, he put his head in his hands.

Claire lay sprawled on the floor of the church, the heat of flames scorching her skin.

Then there was silence.

Looking around, she saw the fire was gone. Ash covered the marble altar. The church pews were empty.

To her right, she heard the same priest say, "As we have discussed, there is no choice but to perform the ritual."

Claire picked herself up off the floor to see the same man and two children standing across from him, their heads bowed. "Through baptism, God will forgive all of your latent sins. You and your children can start new in this holy world."

The man nodded in agreement. The priest motioned to a lipped pool a few feet away–The Well.

The father helped each of the children step over the lip.

They stood looking at their father in fear.

"It will be fine. Just like a bath."

Claire held her breath. The priest moved swiftly, coming behind the man and wrapping his arm around his shoulders. The blood from the slice against the father's throat spattered onto the children's innocent faces. The father struggled, collapsing to the ground. The children screamed. Claire heard the clank of metal. The two children dropped out of sight into the depths of the well. Dropping to her knees, helpless to do anything, Claire watched two of the altar boys lift the body of the father and drop him into the opening of the well.

The fire department arrived. Grant and Shaun stepped out of the way. The men went at the door with a crowbar. The room had filled with smoke.

"You need to get out. We'll handle this," one of the firemen stated.

"We're not leaving," Grant said, struggling to hide the tears in his eyes, visualizing Claire trapped in the flames. It'd been too long.

The fireman touched the door and nodded to the other. Using the crowbars, they wedged them between the hinges of the door, popping them off. "Stand back."

The men counted to three and kicked in the doors. They fell hard, kicking up all of the ash and smoke in the air. The group stood in shock. Ash covered the room, all its contents destroyed. There was no fire.

They heard sobbing. Grant pushed past the men searching through the smoke. He found Claire curled in a ball on the floor. "Claire."

She responded to his voice, reaching out to him. She shook with sobs, wrapping her arms around his neck. "I saw it. I saw what he did, Grant. I saw it all!"

Luke's heart continued to thud loudly in his chest hours after his encounter with the Demon torturing Kelsey James. He reviewed the footage with Dr. Meddleshon and agreed they would try again tomorrow. His head pounded with the words of the Demon. Hopefully, Claire and Shaun's research had uncovered something helpful.

Luke entered the main lobby of the hotel to see Grant and Craig seated at a table in the café. They waved him over.

"Gentlemen, I hope you had a successful evening?"

Grant glanced at Craig. "How did things go with Kelsey James?"

"It's all progressive."

"Were you able to make contact?"

"Yes, but I'm no closer to knowing how to vanquish the Demon," Luke said. "What did Claire and Shaun find?"

Craig's head dipped. Grant shifted into the table.

Luke's stomach churned uneasily. "What happened?"

"There was a fire."

"What?"

Craig and Grant proceeded to convey the entire story of Claire's disappearance through to the discovery of a completely burnt but fireless room. "How's Claire?"

"She's upstairs with Shaun," Craig said.

"When we got back, she locked herself in her bedroom and hasn't come out," Grant said with a deep breath. "We were waiting here to fill you in."

Luke moved.

Grant stood with him. "Whatever she needs."

"Understood," Luke said.

Luke arrived at Claire's door within minutes. It opened a crack when he knocked, revealing Shaun's broad, pale face.

When Shaun opened it wider, Luke walked into the living area of the suite. "Talk to me, Shaun."

CHAPTER EIGHT

Seated cross-legged in the middle of her bed, Claire struggled to focus her mind.

The screaming in her head wouldn't stop.

Two children, covered in their father's blood.

Falling into the Well.

The smell of burning flesh, a screaming corpse begging for mercy.

The knife dripping blood onto the wooden planked floor

Demon eyes staring into her soul, laughing.

Her flesh burning hot and raw.

Water filling her lungs.

Her heart racing in panic.

Calm.

Her body suddenly filled with a warm serenity. Claire opened her eyes and glanced at the clock — it was past 3 AM. Pip lay snoring at the foot of the bed. Claire moved off the bed and toward the door. Turning the knob, she pulled it open to find Luke propped against the wall, seated in the doorway.

Kneeling, Claire crawled into his lap. His arms immediately wrapped securely around her, and she found solace within his embrace. He kissed the top of her head. She said nothing, just snuggled closer.

Luke had known she would come out eventually. She just needed to process what'd happened. He'd settled in as close as he could get to her and prayed, sending her all of his strength and will. The moment she crawled into his lap, Luke's heart sighed in relief. Everything slipped away. The planets aligned the moment she entered his arms. He drifted off, holding her close.

The stench of death curled beneath his nose. Death would have to wait. Something told him twelve-year-old Jenny Ann Waster wasn't ready to die. She still had a full life ahead, despite this particular Demon's insistence she was already gone from this world and trapped in hell.

Jenny Ann's skeletal form lurched from the padded bed in an attempted violent attack against her intended saviors.

"Luke, help me hold her down," the exorcist, Father Daniel called.

Luke immediately followed the priest's instruction. With his arms against Jenny Ann's arms and chest, he gently pushed the small girl back into the mattress. Jenny Ann seemingly relaxed, and Father Daniel started reciting the prayer over the child, inciting the Demon's wrath. The girl once against surged against Luke's hold. Luke repeated the prayer of the priest. The girl twisted and fought against him, releasing a deafening high-pitched scream that seemed to suck up all the air in the room. The noise created agony. The two men instinctively covered their ears. The room erupted into chaos, the air around them turning violent, whipping at the men. Jenny Ann's attention focused on Luke. A low male voice echoed in the room.

"He shall come and mark her with the sight of Heaven and Hell. His flesh to her flesh, she will be enslaved to only him upon the will of the father of darkened light."

The child wailed again, bringing tears of pain to the men, who crumpled. paralyzed.

"She will be water and air. You will suffocate and shrivel, drown and fall from your grace in her name. The darkness will claim your soul."

Another unearthly scream, as if the child were calling out to death himself. A final breath, and the chaos stopped.

Luke's eyes shot open. Guilt, pain, and anguish swept over him in waves. He struggled to remain calm. Claire lay curled against him on the floor. He took a few deep breaths to reclaim his tormented thoughts.

Lifting Claire into his arms, he then carried her to the bed, laid her down, and took position next to her warm body. Once again curling into his chest, Luke wrapped his arms around her soft form, pulling her close. His body was calm, but his mind swirled in debate and questions.

He couldn't ignore the signs any longer. He'd run, but not far enough. It would never be far enough.

"What's wrong?" Claire said, drawing his attention to her eyes, she wiped a tear off his cheek.

"Nothing," Luke said, kissing her fingertips. "Just happy to see those beautiful eyes."

She stared at him for a moment.

Luke wondered if she was going to let it go.

"I know what happened at the church. I saw it."

"Tell me," Luke said, and Claire shifted, recounting her vision. Every word seemed to rip at her, and he struggled to allow her to continue. When she finished, Luke reached out, cupping her cheek in his hand. "Are you all right?"

"No," she said, rising from the bed. "How could I be? It was horrible. I can still feel and smell everything like it's still happening."

"It's not," Luke said, keeping his tone soft and reassuring. "It's the past. You witnessed a horrible event in the past, an event that will hopefully provide us with the answers we need to help Kelsey James and all the people who were brutally murdered to lay at rest."

"Is this how the rest of my life is going to be?" Claire asked, chewing on her thumb.

"I can't tell you what's to come," Luke said, taking her

hand. "What I can tell you is you're amazing. You can handle this and anything else that comes your way. You have this gift for a reason. Let your heart be your guide. You'll figure it out."

Luke received a text from Craig with the address of the evening's investigation. When he arrived, the crew was in full swing, with the two *Finders* SUV's parked out front and the *Finders* van in the driveway. As it was a modern house, he was surprised it was old enough to have developed any activity.

They had two teams for this investigation. One would monitor activity from the van, and the other would do the on-site investigation. Each group consisted of two investigators, a boom—aka soundman—and a cameraman. Mid-shift, just after one, they would switch, giving the option for multiple perspectives and more of a chance to catch something digitally.

Luke joined the teams in setting up cameras, feeding extension cords, setting up various temperature gauges, electronic voice phenomenon devices, and marking pre-existing areas of activity with masking tape on the floor.

It was hours of work, and the sun was hidden away by the time they finished. Luke returned an empty equipment case to the van when he recognized Grant's car.

Grant quickly joined him and the team, stepping into the leadership role.

"Hey, guys, sorry I'm late. Many of you may have heard there was an incident last night at the library involving Claire. She wanted me to assure all of you she is fine and resting comfortably back at the hotel," Grant explained with a smile of reassurance. "Tonight we're investigating the home of Charles and Lily Taylor. They bought the house three years ago and just recently started some renovations, apparently spawning strange phenomenon. They hear whispering, laughing, the sounds of a child playing, the bouncing of a ball up and down the hallway, and the sound of bells like on a child's bike.

"Charles and Lily have no children of their own. Thus, the happenings are becoming unnerving and unsettling. They've asked us to investigate in the hope we can catch some hard evidence and perhaps give them a clue as to who or what is residing in their house. Team A, Brian and Kate, are in-house first. Luke and I will monitor activity in the van with Will. Everyone verify setup is complete and go for lights out and get to work."

Luke followed Grant to the van, where Will, the tech advisor, sat in front of a wall of monitors. From the van, they could see every room in the house during the investigation. "We all set?"

"Looks good here," Will replied.

"Brian and Kate, you good for dark?"

"Good for dark, Grant."

"All teams lights out."

All the lights in the house were turned off, and the investigation began. After a few minutes, Grant looked to Luke. "How's she doing?"

"Struggling, it is a lot to comprehend in a short amount of time. The scene Claire described fits with the remains found near the waterfall but also with the ramblings of our Demon. If the pastor was inadvertently feeding the Demon, thinking he was working in service of the Lord, their souls would have sustained it for centuries."

"We need to go back to the church. I have a call into Sherriff Mingus," Grant said. "Between Kelsey and Claire, there's more there than we thought. The church needs to be our focus."

"Agreed."

"Sorry to interrupt, guys, but something is happening on the second floor," Will said, drawing their attention to the upper right screen. Grant pulled out the walkie-talkie, "Brian, Kate, where are you presently?"

"In the kitchen, why?" Kate responded.

"You mind heading upstairs? We have some activity."

"Going now."

"What did you see?" Luke asked, and Will rewound the recording. He started it again, showing the attic door, a swing down from the ceiling type, beginning to open.

Grant opened the line to Brian, "When you get up there, check the attic door in the ceiling."

"Copy."

When they saw Brian and Kate on the monitor, they watched Brian investigate the door. He acknowledged the opening and pressed against the door. It closed, and he waited. After a moment, it opened to the same spot again. Pulling on the door, he tested the spring, displaying it was loose, and the door could open and close a few inches without a light touch.

"Yup, faulty spring," Will reaffirmed. "Logical explanation. It's amazing to me how many times we find straightforward explanations for these things."

"Good job, Brian," Grant said.

The night went on uneventfully, and it was Team B's turn in the house. Luke, Grant, boom operator Greg, and cameraman Craig started in the kitchen and dining area, where there were reports of whispers and laughter. They sat and did some EVP work trying to catch something audible by asking questions and waiting for answers in the silence.

Grant suggested they go upstairs. "I'd like to check the attic door, just out of curiosity."

"You're the lead here," Luke replied.

The pair found the drop door and tugged on it slightly. The door did creep open like before. Grant pulled a little harder, but it was much more difficult.

Luke heard bells. "Wait."

Grant stopped. Luke pointed up into the attic as the source of the noise. Grant nodded in agreement. Grant tugged on the door, and it groaned, releasing the folding staircase. Luke unfolded the stairs and started upward.

"Here," Grant said, handing him up a mini-cam. "The infra-red is on."

"Thanks," Luke replied, pointing the camera. He saw several boxes, suitcases, and a standing Santa Claus. Hearing movement, he shifted the camera's focus and saw a circular object glowing in the corner. Resting the camera on the ledge, he climbed down the stairs. "Go up and look."

Grant climbed, and Luke waited.

"What is it?" Luke asked.

"A ball maybe? It's about the size of a kickball or exercise ball. I'm going to try and get it," Grant said.

The stairs creaked and then jumped. Luke put his weight on the bottom to keep the stairs from moving further.

"What just happened?" Grant asked.

"Maybe you should come down."

"Wait, it's moving."

"What?"

"The ball, it's rolling toward me." Grant walked back down the steps, his focus on the entrance of the attic. The ball appeared, bouncing down the stairs toward them. The ball glowed flaming red in the camera display. Grant moved out of the way, as did Luke, Greg, and Craig. The group followed the ball. It bounced off the wall and rolled down the hall toward the main staircase. The ball propelled itself down. They followed. The front door stood open, a surprise to them all. The ball rolled out the door, across the porch, and onto the sidewalk, where it stopped.

A dark figure picked up the ball, long hair flying in the wind.

"Claire?" Grant called.

Claire ascended the stairs to the porch, greeting them with a smile.

"What are you doing here?" Grant asked.

Claire examined the ball in her hands and then her gaze met his. "I'm not exactly sure."

Grant looked at Luke. Luke felt a small chill up his spine.

Claire's focus shifted to something or someone beyond Grant. She walked past Grant into the house. Grant moved to follow when the door slammed shut, rattling the windows around the doorframe.

"What the?" Grant muttered, reaching for the door. He twisted the door handle, but the door would not budge. "Luke."

Luke's stomach dropped. He grabbed the handle attempting to open the door, to no avail.

Grant picked up his walkie-talkie, "Will, I need a set of keys to the house."

Claire saw the child just inside the door. He ran up the stairs. She followed until she reached the landing, heard voices from the outside, and turned toward the commotion. The air pushed from her lungs. She hit the opposite wall with a loud thud, as if shoved by a linebacker. Shaken but determined, Claire got to her feet. The child from her bedroom just a few hours before stood only a few feet away. He looked as real as Grant or Luke, startlingly real, especially when she'd awakened to see him standing at the end of her bed.

"I'm sorry." His fear emanated across to her like a cold grip in the night.

"Did you hit me?"

"No. Mother made me."

"What did she make you do?" Claire asked.

The child ran off, disappearing into a room at the end of the hall. Claire took a breath, seeing the cabling, devices, cameras, and equipment strewn through the house. It would catch everything, even her talking to herself. What the hell was she doing there? *This child – spirit or ghost or whatever – needs help. He came to me, and I – Shit, do I even know how to help him? Luke will know what to do, right?*

She turned to the landing, knowing she should get Luke and Grant. Something dashed just out of her vision, and she twirled to face whatever it was. There was nothing. The same thing happened again, something moving just out of her view. She turned back, and her vision focused. A woman appeared, her hair twisted into a tight knot at the top of her head. Her mouth opened, and a shrill scream burst from her lips. Claire fell to her knees at the sheer hatred thrust upon her senses — black, cold, and deep, like the waters of the well.

Grant approached the truck with Luke.

"Can you see anything?" Craig asked.

"No, the cameras keep moving or fuzzing out, but we can hear everything."

"What's happening?"

A shrill deafening scream jolted the entire team. Will ripped off his headphones. Grant and Luke looked to the house.

"What the hell was that?" Grant asked.

"Was that Claire?" Craig asked.

"I have no idea," Will said. "Whatever it was just blew out all the microphones."

"Jesus," Grant said, rubbing the top of his bald head in awe and concern. "We need to get in there."

"Keys!" Luke said. Will tossed them across the van to him. Luke rushed to the door. Saying a small prayer, he blessed the lock and inserted the key. The door clicked.

Claire opened her eyes to darkness, confused as to her whereabouts. Immediate panic took hold. *Stop, take a breath.*

"We're safe here," a small voice said in the darkness.

"What's your name?"

"Tim."

"Hi, Tim. My name is Claire," she said in a very melodic, steady tone. "Did you bring me here?" Claire waited for a response. The long pause caused her panic to grow again. "Tim, are you still here?"

"Yes."

"Can you tell me who attacked me in the hallway?"

"Mother."

"Your mother?"

"Yes."

"Is she the reason you're still here, Tim?"

"She doesn't want to leave. She's scared of going to Hell."

Claire searched the darkness in vain, looking for any shape or shadow. "Is there a Hell?"

"I don't know," Tim said, his voice small and distant. "Mother believes we're going to Hell. She won't let us leave. She hates the Taylors. They keep changing everything. When Mother gets angry, bad things happen."

"Is there something I can do to help your Mom move on? Something I can do to reassure her, Tim?"

Luke, Grant, and Craig pushed their way inside the house.

"I'll take the kitchen, Luke, you take the living room. Craig, stay here and keep filming," Grant said.

Luke entered the living room, walking through quickly in his search for Claire. He stopped surveying the room, his hand resting on the hearth of the fireplace. He glanced at the intricate woven design before hearing Grant enter the room.

"Anything?" Grant asked Luke, shaking his head. "Let's check upstairs."

The temperature in the small area dropped. Claire's body tensed.

Something is off.

"Tell me how I can help you."

"Can you take my hand?" the child asked.

Claire's heart raced. *No, don't. It's lying,* a small voice whisper in her ear.

"Who are you? What do you want?" Claire asked aloud.

The room's air turned stagnant. Claire tried not to cough.

Air . . . need fresh air

The room spun. Claire felt a heated breath at her back. An unfurled growl erupted in her ear, halting her movement. Throbbing pain spiked behind her left eye. The distant shrill of a scream resounded, growing louder with every second. Claire could feel the pressure of her blood pounding through her body with every heartbeat. *Breathe.* The need for air sent her into a panic, her lungs refusing to fill.

Luke and Grant reached the top of the stairs. A scream echoed off the walls, causing the two men to step back in concern. "Claire!" they both yelled, looking for a response.

"Where's it coming from?" Craig called up, shifting the camera.

Grant descended the stairs. Luke remained at the top. They

waited for another scream but heard nothing. Luke felt a brush of icy air across his neck. He turned, and his boot bumped something. The blue ball they'd followed out of the attic and down the stairs to Claire sat at his feet.

"Grant," Luke said, his focus fixated on the ball.

"What?" Grant called, ascending the stairs to join him.

Within a breath, the ball started rolling. They glanced at each other and then followed. The ball continued its path down the hallway and stopped.

"Claire?" Grant called.

A *crack* drew their attention to the ceiling. Both men looked up. Another *crack* sounded, followed by a low growl echoing off the walls.

Luke realized they were only a few feet from the attic entrance. Suddenly, Claire fell through the ceiling like a sledgehammer through the drywall. Luke's instincts kicked in automatically positioning himself to catch her before she hit the floor. She dropped into his outstretched arms, gasping and coughing. Luke's focus shot upward. His feet stayed rooted to the floor. Two red eyes and a skeletal face stared down at him from the darkness above.

A prayer fell from his lips. "I armor myself today with the power of the Most Holy Trinity, in the oneness of God, Creator of the universe. I armor myself today with the baptism of Christ, His crucifixion, and resurrection, His ascension and glorious second coming." The Demon stared down at them, screaming a deathly wail.

Claire swung out of Luke's arms, taking a stance beside him. Craig appeared in the distance camera pointed at all the action.

"Stay behind me," Luke told her.

"No, I want to face it," Claire said defiantly, her hand curling around his.

"I armor myself today with God's guidance to direct me,

God's might to sustain me, God's wisdom to instruct me, God's word to give me speech, God's shield to protect me, God's army to defend me against the snares of demons, against the lure of vices, against all who plot me harm," Luke said, the strength of the words flooding his veins, the adrenaline giving him power and confidence.

"I invoke all these virtues today against every hostile and merciless power that may assail me, against the incantations of false prophets, against the black laws of heathenism, against the false laws of heresy, against the deceits of idolatry, against every art and spell that binds the soul to evil."

Claire and Grant repeated his words as Luke completed each line. The entity bellowed again, plunging the hallway into darkness. Hearing a thud a few feet ahead of him, Luke assumed the entity had jumped from the attic onto the floor.

"Christ guard me today against every poison, burning, drowning, and fatal wounding" The odor of the room changed to sulfur and a foulness he could not describe. Luke's hand raised against the unseen force. "Christ be with me, Christ be behind me, Christ be within me, Christ be beside me, Christ to win me." A scalding wind whipped around them. Luke stood firm, Claire's hand never leaving his grasp. "Christ to comfort and restore me, Christ to be where danger threatens, Christ be in the hearts of those around me, forevermore."

The house went silent. The lights in the room flickered back on. Luke stumbled against the wall, using it for support, his knees shaking and breath trembling. Claire's lithe form fell against his chest. They both slid down to the floor to recover from the battle.

"Luke, Claire, are you all right?" Grant asked, looking at the pair from his position on the floor. Luke assisted Claire up. The trio met beneath the hole in the ceiling.

"I think we're okay," Claire answered, looking to Luke.

"What the hell just happened?" Grant asked, looking to Claire.

"I-I honestly don't know," Claire said.

Grant, Luke, Craig, and Claire regrouped in the living room. Craig continued filming. Claire attempted to calm her frayed nerves and process what had happened.

What did happen? The distracting buzzing in her brain would not cease, and she struggled to focus. It was then she realized Grant was repeatedly saying her name.

"Claire," Grant said, and she met his concerned gaze. "Let's start from the beginning. What brought you here? Why are you not at the hotel?"

Claire opened her mouth to start talking but hesitated. She rose from the couch, needing space.

"Just tell us what's going on."

Claire continued to struggle, her focus swirling like a leaf in the wind. A golden glow emanated from the corner of the room. The child she'd seen in her bedroom and the woman who screamed at her stood smiling. The mother wrapped a loving arm around the child. The child waved to Claire.

"Don't be afraid," the child said before the light sharpened and then disappeared.

Claire took a breath before turning to face Grant and Luke. "The mother and son that lived here before were causing the problems. They've moved on."

"How do you know that?"

"I just saw them, and they said goodbye," Claire replied, watching the expressions of Grant and Luke closely. Both men remained silent. "The boy appeared at the foot of my bed at the hotel. He led me here, where I met you both on the porch. I had no idea this was where he was leading me."

"How exactly did he lead you to the house?" Luke asked.

"He whispered the address in my ear, and I took an Uber," Claire replied, and the group chuckled a little.

"What happened while you were talking to us on the porch?" Grant asked, bringing the focus back to the conversation. "You seemed distracted."

"I saw the little boy running from something inside the house. I was concerned so I went inside. I thought you were both behind me," Claire explained.

"Then what happened?" Grant asked, and Claire recounted the rest of the experience until the moment she fell from the ceiling.

"I don't think whatever was with me in the attic was associated with the child and his mother. The little boy warned me about — whatever it was — and helped me escape from the attic. The entity Demon thing attacked me. The boy told me how to push through the drywall to escape."

"What kind of attack?" Luke asked.

"It's difficult to describe. I felt like I was underwater. Everything was blocked out. I couldn't breathe."

"Sounds like a paranormal bubble."

"A what?"

"It's just like she explained. A bubble of paranormal energy meant to isolate and focus an attack on a single individual — in this case, Claire." Luke turned to her. "You don't think the entity you encountered was previously present in this house?"

"No, I don't. I think the entity we just encountered is the same Demon residing inside Kelsey James and responsible for pushing me down the well at Crestwater Church."

CHAPTER NINE

Grant escorted Claire back to the hotel while Luke and Craig wrapped up the shoot . . . more like Craig wrapped up the investigation, and Luke nodded, his mind preoccupied with recent events. The time and work moved quickly. They headed back to the hotel in a few hours.

"What happened back there?" Craig asked, breaking the silence of the truck.

"What do you mean?" Luke responded, realizing he was running on autopilot.

"I just . . . I've never seen anything before like Claire described and then the attack. On top of finding her in the middle of a room of ash last night, I guess I'm in shock."

"That's a good way to describe it."

"The evidence we capture has always been on the cusp of concrete, never solid, and always just a hair of unbelievable, but this — what's been happening the past few days is beyond comprehension. How did we go from a gray area to real?"

"Craig—"

"I just witnessed a woman I've known for years walk into a house and not only uncover the source of a haunting but then summarily get violently and physically attacked by a Demon."

Luke didn't have an answer, and they spent the remainder of the trip in silence.

Arriving at the hotel, they found Grant and Claire in the dining area. Luke and Craig joined them, taking a seat at the table.

"Wrap go okay?" Grant asked.

"Without a hitch. How about here?"

"Claire and I are decompressing."

"That was all pretty intense. I still don't know what to make of it," Craig said, looking at Claire. "Are you okay?"

"I'm fine," Claire said, glancing at Grant. "A little rattled, but I'll survive."

"Has anything like that ever happened to you before?" Craig asked.

"No, it was a first."

"It is wild how this stuff works sometimes. It makes you wonder what triggers an event like that."

"Did you get it done?" Grant asked Craig.

"Yeah, everything has been uploaded to the cloud and is ready to go," Craig replied, rubbing his hands together with a smile.

Claire wandered off to the coffee station, and Luke followed. He found her filling up a cup with fresh coffee.

"I'm no expert, but coffee is probably not the best thing to be drinking after the night you've had," Luke commented.

"It's decaf," Claire said, taking another sip. "I just needed something warm."

"Haven't been able to shake the chill yet?"

"Not yet," she said, staring at the floor. "I honestly wonder if I'll ever be warm again."

The somberness of the statement shocked him, and he instinctively stepped closer.

Claire's eyes were distant and haunting. "You saw it, didn't you? You looked up and saw it, just like I did." The conviction in Claire's eyes told him she wasn't going to let him off the hook.

"Yes, I saw it," Luke admitted.

"Tell me I'm not losing my mind or going crazy," Claire

said, the heat of her body warming his chest. With those sparkling eyes shining up at him, he couldn't ignore the stirring of his soul.

"No, you are very sane," Luke said, brushing a stray hair from her cheek and tucking it behind her ear. "We're going to figure this out."

"How?" she asked, her eyes studying him.

"The way you've been doing already with something you're very talented in, research, interviews, history of the land, the church, the people, and the individual experiences. We take the data, form a hypothesis, and a plan to test it. From there, it's trial and error."

"Sounds like a lengthy process."

"Sometimes it is," Luke replied, relaxing into the conversation. "An investigation can take months or even years to identify what's happening at a location or to an individual."

"How can you tell the difference?"

"It can be difficult. A good indicator is if the person leaves the location and the attacks continue. The entity has attached itself, or a deeper psychosis is present."

"Attached itself like a parasite and a host?"

"Exactly."

"Why?"

"Why what?"

"Why would an entity attach itself to a person? What do they get out of it?"

"Power," Luke explained. "When an entity attaches to a living person, it feeds off their energy, emotions, and soul, consuming all the precious nutrients needed to sustain their life force, making the Demon stronger and bigger, enabling them to create more havoc."

"They feed until the person dies?"

"Many times, yes, or until the entity finds a more appetizing host."

"Like someone with a stronger life force or abilities."

"Yes," Luke replied, watching her crystal eyes as she processed the information.

"Then what?"

"Vanquish it back to wherever it came from."

"Good answer," Claire said with a small smile.

"What?"

"I was just thinking about something Shaun said to me about being a living superhero."

"You are," Luke said.

"Yeah? In all of the superhero movies I've seen, the hero can destroy the villain, not just vanquish it to live another day," Claire said. "I'm quickly learning real life is nothing like the movies."

"Correct, it's not. It's not your job to vanquish anything. You're a medium."

"I don't even know what that means."

"I think you've watched enough movies to know what it means to be a medium."

"Okay, maybe I have a glimmer of what you're talking about, but this isn't how it's supposed to happen. People do not just fall down wells perfectly normal and come out Lorraine Warren."

"Slow down and take a breath. A lot has happened. I would be a little freaked out too," Luke said, taking her hand.

"A little freaked out? I'm much more than a little freaked . . ." Her eyes widened and her hand turned cold. "There's a man in a hat with glasses and a scruffy beard. He's in his late sixties. I can feel a tightening around my neck, pain in the back of the spine. There's rain and —"

"Claire, stop," Luke said, yanking his hand away. She swayed on her feet. He wrapped his arm around her waist to steady her balance.

"A child, a little girl, named . . ."

"Claire, are you all right?" Grant said, joining them by the coffee station.

"That's the current debate," Claire said, looking to Luke.

"We need to talk," Grant said. "The sheriff left me a voicemail. We are cleared to investigate the church tomorrow night. Given everything that's happened, we need a plan."

They decided to brainstorm and regroup in the morning. Grant dialed his phone and walked away.

"Who's the guy with the beard?' Claire asked, the images still a swirl of color in her mind's eye.

"You look tired," Luke said, his hand resting on the small of her back. "How have you been sleeping?"

The warmth of his touch sent shots of reassurance through her body, relaxing her even more. "Not great. I answered your question. How about you answer mine?" A flash of doubt erupted, and her heart raced.

"I will, eventually, just not at this moment," he replied, taking her coffee and handing her a glass of water.

Honestly, feeling a little drunk and not having the energy to fight him, she mentally marked the topic for discussion later. "Are you always this attentive?"

A lopsided grin ebbed his chiseled features. "Only with women who have almost drowned, been strangled, and or experienced paranormal phenomenon within forty-eight hours," Luke said as a cold wisp of air brushed her neck.

Unable to break the intense stare of his deep brown eyes, Claire reminded herself to take a breath. "Sounds like a pretty exclusive group."

"It is," Luke replied.

Her stomach warmed and her cheeks burned. "I'm exhausted and going to bed," Claire said. "Thanks for everything."

"My pleasure," Luke replied.

Claire made it to her room, fed and watered Pip, and exhaustion settled in. Grabbing her pajamas, she dressed and crawled beneath the covers. Warm blackness seeped through, and she gladly fell in.

Thudding boomed against her ears. The warmth of Pip consoled her mind, and she willed away the distraction. It stopped.

The clanging of metal came next. Chains, hitting, sliding, and falling. A chilling unease came over her, and she shifted, rolling onto her side. Beside her in bed, Luke Melloy lay peacefully sleeping. Warmth and adoration erased the chill, sending tingles of delight into her stomach. His eyes opened, and he smiled. His hand stroked the side of her face, and she closed her eyes.

Moments later, Claire's eyes opened in the dark, the feeling of safety and warmth still encompassing her mind, body, and soul. After a moment she noticed Pip's absence in the bed. "Pippy?" She heard a whimper and jumped from the bed. Her eyes took a second to focus, and then she saw Pip in the next room, five feet off the ground, hanging by the neck. She screamed at the top of her lungs, lunging to go to him, but was shoved by an invisible force to the floor.

"No!" Rising to her feet, she ran to help him and was once again shoved back. She heard knocking on the door and Luke's voice. "Luke, help, please help!" Claire fought to reach Pip. The invisible force kept her away. She heard a thudding against the door. The same invisible force yanked the spiked metal leash tighter around Pip's neck.

"God, no! Please, no!"

The door frame cracked, and Luke and Grant fell into the room. They both saw the dog hanging in mid-air. Before anyone could act, Pip fell to the ground with a thud, and the force holding Claire released. Claire threw herself across the room, taking the limp animal into her arms. "No, please, baby, please."

"What do we do?" Grant asked.

"Go get the truck and meet us out front." Luke moved past Claire into the bedroom and returned with a blanket. Wrapping the blanket firmly around the dog, he lifted him into his arms. Claire took a breath following Luke down the elevator and out to Grant, waiting in the car.

The nearest Animal Hospital took Pip in for an examination as soon as they arrived. Grant, Luke, and Claire paced the floor in silence.

"Ms. Westin?" a woman in scrubs said, exiting the examination area.

"Is he okay?" Claire asked.

"Pip is doing just fine. He has some bruising around his collar and a few cracked ribs, but he seems okay. We want to keep him overnight to be sure there's no internal bleeding and no lasting effects from the strangulation. Barring any complications, you can take him home tomorrow."

"Oh, thank God," Claire said, looking to Grant and Luke.

"Would you like to see him?" the vet asked.

"Yes, please, yes," Claire replied.

She escorted Claire into the back where Pip lay in a large kennel padded with blankets and pillows. His ribs were wrapped in bandages, and Claire almost lost it when he opened his eyes, looking at her wearily.

"He's on pain medication. He's going to be sleepy, but he'll know you're here," the vet said. "Don't stay too long. He needs to rest."

"Thank you for everything."

"My pleasure, Ms. Westin," she replied before walking away.

Claire got down on the floor to be in Pip's line of sight. His tail moved slightly. "Hey, Bubba. Momma is going to fix this,

I promise." Claire gently stroked his head, tears streaming down her cheeks. "Don't you worry. The doctor says you need to stay here for a while, but I'll be back, I promise. You rest. Momma loves you, Pippy."

It took everything in her to leave the hospital. Grant left her and Luke alone to get the car. After a moment, the dam burst, and she openly sobbed. Luke's arms wrapped around her, and Claire hid her face against his chest. Shaking with agony and fear, she didn't know how to stop.

Luke attempted to console her, his hands threading through her hair. "It's gonna be okay."

"Why is this happening?" Claire asked through broken sobs.

Before Luke could answer, Grant, pulled up with the truck. Luke opened the back door and ushered her inside. His instinct was to climb in next to her, but he held back. Instead, he shut the door and jumped in the passenger front, giving Claire the space she needed to process what happened.

A thickening silence hung in the air during the drive back to the hotel, broken only by a random sniffle from Claire. There were no words for the situation. Stiffly tense in the passenger's seat, Luke worked hard to actively suppress the anger and concern coursing through his veins. Claire's tears felt like acid in his heart, painful and sharp.

As they approached the hotel, Grant was the first to speak. "Claire, I'll talk to the hotel about securing your room. I think it would be safest for you to stay with Luke for the night."

Luke looked at his friend in surprise before nodding in agreement. Then he turned to Claire, who nodded as well.

Grant dropped them at the front entrance. "Try and get some sleep."

"Will do," Luke replied and escorted Claire into the hotel.

"Are you sure you're okay with this arrangement?" As she met his gaze, her exhaustion was undeniable, and he felt her hand slide into his.

"Yes."

The now familiar warmth of her touch shot indescribable need through his body. Cherishing her hand in his, he gently squeezed, and they walked into the hotel together.

Luke escorted Claire to her room. The busted door was propped against the wall in the hallway. Claire entered, and Luke followed. She released his hand. His heart unexpectedly wept. He waited, scanning the room for anything to distract his mind. Claire disappeared for only a moment and then re-appeared with an armful of clothing and a computer bag. She scurried from the room.

They walked the short distance to Luke's. He unlocked the door and opened it for Claire to enter.

She stepped in, laying down her bag out of the way.

"I'll take the couch. You can have the bed," Luke offered.

Claire nodded in response before walking into the bathroom and closing the door.

Luke removed his shirt, then opened the closet door and tugged the extra blanket from the top shelf. With his mind heavy with worry about Claire, he moved into the bedroom to grab a pillow, just as Claire opened the door of the bathroom. He tossed the pillow onto the couch, facing Claire.

She was still clearly in shock and listless. He brushed her chin with his fingertip, leading her vast emotion-filled eyes to meet his gaze. A broken breath escaped her lips, her soft hand resting on his chest. The tip of her finger gently traced the golden cross hanging just below his collar.

The air in his lungs escaped, his heart racing with warmth and excitement. He moved his hand to frame the side of her cheek, his fingers pushing into her soft hair. Reluctance swept over him. His thoughts were swimming, making it nearly impossible to breathe. "Claire—"

She must have recognized his hesitation. Instead of pulling away, her soft pink lips met his with a tender passion.

Luke's senses ignited, his body surging with desire. He took control of the kiss, cradling her head in his hands, angling her mouth to deepen his exploration.

To kiss her forever would not be long enough. She trembled in his arms. He worked to kiss away all her fears. His mouth not leaving hers, they walked to the bed. Luke eased her down in his arms. Her luscious heated body pressed up against him.

Her mouth was eager, ripe, and willing. Their tongues toyed and teased, pushing Luke's desires higher. His mouth wandered, tracing the contour of her throat. A shiver rocked him when her nails scraped his exposed ribs. He felt her fiery mouth on his collar bone and his chest. Luke groaned at the barrier of cloth between his hands and her silken flesh. The scent of her was intoxicating, and his groin surged.

Claire shifted and lifted her shirt over her head, revealing her smooth silken skin.

His focus went to her bra, and her hands went to his pants. Revealing her breasts, Luke quickly took a supple nipple into his mouth. Circling the engorged bud with his tongue, he heard her gasp and low moan. He took the affirmation and continued to nip, lick, and tease her nipples. She aggressively tugged at his pants, and he trapped her wrists in his hands above her head. Hovering his mouth just over her hers, he kicked off his pants before crushing their mouths together. Moving his body to the side, he held both of her hands with his one. His other hand moved down her stomach, slipping beneath her pajama shorts.

The smooth skin beneath his fingers sent spikes of electricity straight to his groin. Blindly searching for Claire's clit, he found it swollen and teased it with the pad of his finger. Her hips shifted with his caress. He used her increasing wetness to slip two fingers down and into her pussy. As he gently pushed into the entry, she gasped. He deliberately slid in and out of her depths, his need to be inside her body surged to an uncomfortable level. Releasing her hands, Luke covered her sculpted shoulders, neck, and chest in kisses. Continuing to move his hand in an out of her pussy, he teased her nipples, unable to get enough of the hardened buds between his lips.

Slowly working his way down her body, Luke placed a kiss just below her belly button and pulled his fingers out of her warmth. He tugged at her shorts. The valley between her legs revealed a pink, moist, and perfect pussy. As he began with a bold swipe of his tongue, her back arched, pushing her wet pussy hard against his mouth. She entwined her fingers into his hair, and the room filled with her gasps and moans. His tongue encircled and drenched her clit. He worked his fingers again into her pussy, and she writhed against his hand, lost in her pleasure. After a few moments of his ministrations, the pleasure rippled through her, hot and wet. She cried out his name, tugging on his hair before melting into the cushion of the bed.

Luke kissed his way up her body, cherishing every touch. Her hands still in his hair, he heard her sigh. He covered her face and lips with soft, tender kisses. Her hands trailed down his back around to his stomach and pushed into his boxers, wrapping around his hardened cock. She stroked him slowly. His hips moved with the cadence of her hands. He struggled to remain in control. She breathed in his ear. He groaned in frustration. He pulled on his mental reins but quickly lost the battle.

Unable to hold back his desire, Luke rose from the bed. Discarding his boxers, he dug into his bag, pulling out a condom. Ripping it open, he wasted no time in rolling it over his engorged cock. Claire lay waiting for him. He gulped back his shock. The woman lying before him was so beautiful and so amazing. Rejoining her on the bed, Luke leaned forward, placing a hard, deep, and desire-filled kiss on her perfect pink lips.

She opened to him, inviting him into her mouth, speaking without words. He lay between her legs, teasing her folds and covering his cock in her juices. She pushed her hips upward, and he teased her entrance, rubbing without entering. Claire groaned before he pressed himself into the heated center of her body. They both gasped in pleasure at the union. It was all Luke could do to remain in control and not just explode within her scorching heat. He moved inside her, and she matched him thrust for thrust.

Claire's fingers entwined within his, and they moved together in a raw rhythm of need and desire. He fought the building sensation and his need for release, struggling to hold on just a little longer. Her pussy tightened around his shaft, milking him. The incredible deliciousness of the sensation pushed him over the edge. Luke grasped her hips, pulling her hard into his final thrust.

His body tensed, blood pumping hot before his cock melted inside her beautiful body. Luke's arms gave out. He rolled onto his side, taking her with him. Trying to catch his breath, he pulled her against his chest, placing a kiss on her forehead. Exhausted, Luke listened to the sound of her steady breathing until he was sure she was asleep and then allowed his mind to relax and drift away.

"He shall come and mark her with the sight of Heaven and Hell. His flesh to her flesh, she will be enslaved to only he upon the will of the father of darkened light."

The child wailed again bringing tears of pain to the men who crumpled paralyzed.

"She will be water and air. You will suffocate and shrivel, drown

and fall from your grace in her name. The darkness will claim your soul."

Jenny Anne's face contorted and twisted, then released a howling scream.

As he shook from his sleep, Luke's vision cleared, and his heart calmed. Spooned against him, Claire lay in sweet slumber, and he took a breath. He didn't believe in prophecies or demonic rants, but the words swirled to the front of his consciousness. Even the slightest chance the Demon was talking about Claire sparked a fire in his gut. A desperate need to protect her from harm undeniably rolled into his chest.

He wondered what time it was. Slowly turning onto his back, he reached for his phone. One PM, not bad. Claire shifted slightly, and a wafting scent of peach met his nose, electrifying his body. Fighting the need to pull her closer, caress her soft skin, and make love to her again, he begged his body to calm. He stared at the ceiling and tried to distract his body and mind, to no avail. He needed to get out of there. Silently rising from the bed, he tugged on his running clothes. Leaving a note on the table, he sent a text to Grant before heading to the park.

Claire sighed inwardly at the thought of consciousness, fighting her separation from the warm cocoon of safety. Soft breath at the back of her neck and strong hands kneaded her lower back coaxing her from her place of solace. Slumber kept her silent. His touch felt good. She yearned for it, craved it. Her body melted into the pleasure, her senses aroused and needing his attention. A gentle hand dipped just beneath the waist of her pajama pants, caressing her hip before it slid around to her stomach. The intimate touch made Claire sleepily turn into the heat of his touch.

Met by cold emptiness, Claire's eyes shot open, Luke's name at the edge of her lips. She pulled back, the full weight of reality demolishing the fantasy. Shaken and confused, she scrambled from the warmth of the bed, jumping to her feet. Catching her breath, she convinced herself it was a dream. Her thoughts swung to Pip, and tears unconsciously fell from her eyes. Pulling on her clothes and grabbing her room key, she went to the door, then saw a note propped on the desk. Claire stopped.

I hope you slept well. Went for a run, see you when I get back.

The warmth of the words filled her chest. She pondered Luke's face in her mind. Exiting the room, she walked down the hall to her room. Greeted by a broken door frame and a slightly open entry door, she pushed into the room, reliving the horror of the previous evening. Tossing the awful memory away, Claire made a beeline to the closet and grabbed some clothes before locking herself in the bathroom.

CHAPTER TEN

Sheriff Marty Mingus stood facing the camera against a backdrop of jagged edges and swollen gray skies. His face looked weathered and exhausted.

Claire sympathized with the man. His small storybook town had just shattered into one hundred and fifty-two pieces. They'd unwittingly uncovered a dark secret, and the quiet town would never be the same.

"The Crestwater Wyoming Sheriff's department in conjunction with the US National Forensics Department and the Wyoming State Anthropological Society has identified a total of one hundred and fifty-two separate corpses. Fifty-eight of the bodies were female adults. Sixty-three bodies were children under the age of twelve. The remaining thirty-one were adult males. Carbon testing has dated the average age of the remains in a range of a hundred to a hundred and twenty-five years. Due to the age of the remains, we will be unable to identify all of the victims. All inquiries into the remains are to be directed to the Wyoming Anthropological Society," he stated in a low but clear tone. "Due to the circumstances surrounding the recent events involving Kelsey James, we have authorized the *Finders* Paranormal Investigation Team to do a thorough and complete investigation of the premises. All other persons found on the premises will be considered trespassers and will be prosecuted to the fullest extent of the law."

"Will the *Finders* investigation results be shared with the public?" a random reporter asked.

"After the investigation, all evidence collected will be

reviewed. A decision will be made by the sheriff's office whether or not to add it as part of the public record. That is all," the sheriff concluded before stepping away from the camera and through the barrage of reporters. He stepped through the doors of the church and out of sight.

"Get out of there and back to the truck," Claire said over the walkie-talkie, watching the entire scene from the safety of the *Finders* media van. Sighing, she glanced at all the monitoring and equipment, knowing this would be her secure home for the next twelve hours.

She, Grant, Luke, and the team had decided the investigation of Crestwater Church would be done by standard operating protocols with no exceptional circumstances, save one. Claire was not for any reason allowed inside the church. She had reluctantly agreed to the restriction, not wanting to put herself or anyone on the team in harm's way. Shaun would be joining the investigation and promised to be her eyes and ears, not to mention the overwhelming amount of equipment, cameras, sound recording devices, and other various gadgets the team was setting up throughout the building. It was an ample space to cover. Claire flew in extra support and equipment for the occasion. They were going to do this right.

While everyone else was setting up, Claire spent the day doing her job, getting B-Roll, corralling the marketing team, and communicating with the corporate office on status, timelines, and risk analysis. They didn't want this to turn out to be another *Al Capone's Vault*. Claire's gut told her it would not be the case, and in the end, they would probably have a bombshell of a story. The ramifications terrified and excited her at the same moment. No need to get ahead of herself. One moment at a time.

She queued the footage she'd taken of their tech specialist Will explaining the ghost hunting plan.

"Tell me about the teams," Claire heard herself say.

Will nodded, took a breath, and began, "On this investigation, each team consists of five people — a team leader, two investigators, a cameraman, and a boom or sound operator. Three teams entered the church at a time, led by either Grant, Shaun, or Luke. Each has a designated area to investigate. The investigation goes in shifts of fifty minutes to one hundred minutes, depending on the size of the area. Different teams will have the opportunity to explore the different areas. Paranormal phenomena don't happen on cue. There can be several hours of inactivity. Paranormal investigating is a stakeout, sometimes boring and uneventful, but the investigators always need to be fresh, alert, and ready."

"Great job, Will, as always," Claire praised. Will was the quiet one of the team — the nerd but always pleasant and helpful. A short, stout man, he reminded her of the famous actor and director Kevin Smith. Whenever she had questions about tech, she knew Will would have the answers. "Okay, now let's talk about evidence collection and tech."

Will nodded again, took a breath and began. "For tonight's investigation, each investigator has a standard pack of equipment, a high-powered flashlight so they don't trip over stuff, an EVP monitor, or electronic voice phenomenon recorder. It picks up sounds not usually audible to the human ear. We use it when in an EVP session, where we ask questions and see if we can capture both audible and inaudible responses. They are also equipped with an EMF meter, which monitors electrostatic activity, and a special K2 meter, monitoring changes in the electromagnetic fields but also alerting us to temperature changes in the area, helping us to identify hot and cold spots."

"Why are monitoring temperature and electromagnetic fields important to the investigation?"

"The theory behind the monitoring of temperature in haunted locations is that an entity absorbs the surrounding energy in order to manifest, creating a cold spot in the area where it exists. The electromagnetic field will show a spike in the event a spirit or entity is in the room. We've been able to follow the spikes with the EMF detector and follow an entity from room to room like a trail of paranormal breadcrumbs. We've also been successful in communication with spirits utilizing the K2 meter because of the lights. We've had EVP sessions where we recorded visual responses on the K2 meter when asking an entity or spirit questions. They can control the intensity of the electromagnetic field, allowing for yes or no responses through the meter."

"What else do they have?"

"The teams also have a special infra-red camera, which we also use to monitor hot and cold temperatures, visually recording the occurrences. All of these things assist in documenting and providing corroborative evidence in the event we do encounter an entity or spirit."

"Anything else?"

"There are their five senses and even a sixth sense. While all our equipment helps to guide and collect evidence, nothing compares to the human experience. Our highly trained team utilizes their human skills and reflexes to identify when something is off. Nothing like a gut instinct to send us in the right direction. Ghost hunting is a developed skill with time and practice."

"Perfect, Will. That's a wrap."

She heard a knock on the truck door before it opened, and she saw Luke's handsome face when it did. Her stomach's butterflies flurried at the sight of him, and snippets of their passionate lovemaking the night before flashed in her mind. Thankfully the truck was dark, hiding the rising crimson she could feel in her cheeks.

"Hey, gorgeous, how did the sheriff's interview go?" he asked, stepping up into the van and closing the door.

"Good, the media hoard should start thinning out in about an hour. Plenty of time for lights out," Claire replied. "How are things going inside?"

Luke smiled and chuckled. "You don't want to know."

"Really, what's wrong?"

"The power keeps going out. No matter what Craig and Kate do, it is not cooperating."

"Crap."

"It's not uncommon, but annoying none-the-less," Luke said. "The good news is the sheriff was able to give us some more insight into the building. We found the entrance to the catacombs beneath the church."

"Catacombs?"

"Yeah, apparently there is a tunnel leading to the bottom of the waterfall."

"Would've been nice to know when we were stuck down there."

"Agreed. Grant decided we'll send teams down with the heat monitoring equipment and see what we find," Luke said.

"Hopefully, no more bodies."

"Don't jinx it," Luke said.

"Sorry."

"How are you holding up?" Luke asked, taking her hand in his.

"I'm okay," Claire replied. "I called the vet. Pip is doing great. The vet hospital is good with keeping him tonight."

"Good, I'm glad to hear he's going to be okay, and that he won't be here," Luke said. "While I wouldn't mind him being your guard dog, I know if anything happened to him, you would be devastated."

Claire nodded, tears welling in her eyes as she internally relived the sight of her beloved companion hanging in mid-air, struggling for life all over again. She wiped away the wetness and looked away.

"Hey, he's okay, and he's safe," Luke said, moving closer to her. "It's gonna be okay. We're going to get through this night, and then we are outta here."

"Right," she said. "It's the getting through the night part I'm worried about," Claire said.

"You understand why we—I—don't want you in there. It's not because you can't handle yourself or would do anything wrong."

"I know," she said. "I get it, and I'm good with it. After seeing what happened, I would be okay if I never set foot inside ever again."

"Claire, this Demon is targeting you. They're not like the movies. They can do things, manipulate you, what you see, hear, and experience. There are no rules or limits to their power. There is no magical potion or incantation to stop them. We can't destroy them. All we can do is fight against them and banish them back to Hell. They are—for lack of a better term—gods. You need to be careful, watchful, and alert. If you need anything, if anything feels off or you feel threatened, you need to tell us. Myself, Grant or Shaun. Okay?"

"Yes," Claire nodded.

"Promise me."

"I promise," she replied, and he kissed the top of her hand.

"I'd better get back," Luke said, rising from his chair.

"Luke," Claire called, and he turned toward her. She leaned forward, kissing him lovingly. "Be safe, and thank you."

"My pleasure," he said, kissing her again before exiting the truck.

Luke shut the door of the van, knowing even metal and steel wouldn't be able to protect Claire if the Demon decided to attack. He would need to stop it before it got the chance. The skies were threatening and dark. Not a good sign. More than one kind of storm headed their way. As he stared at the front of the church, a deep knot of dread dropped into his stomach. The last time he was here, he hadn't even noticed the front of the church.

The Burning Beacon of Wyoming stood tall at the top of the hill. The church's face overlooked its congregation. Their sins would be seen by the church no matter where they committed them. A burnt redwood exterior seemed soaked in blood in a constant reminder of the rule of God and eternal punishment. Rebuilt several times, it appeared the front had always remained preserved. Always watching, no matter its state. The expansive stones steps were weathered, uneven, and rolled beneath a person's feet. The effect was utterly subliminal, the feeling of being put off balance even before entering. Every detail from the location, the blood redwood exterior, the uneven steps, to the large windows all was engineered to both illuminate and instill fear, to both create and destroy shadows.

No more.

He reentered the church, and the quiet of the wilderness disappeared in a flurry of activity. They'd called in nearly twenty investigators to help with the setup. Bunches of cords twisted and curled through the building looking like a nest of snakes. Free-standing high-powered lights illuminated the ancient dilapidated building. Despite the wooden exterior, the inside was mostly local stone and well-placed marble. Quite beautiful in its day, the rocks were now moss-covered and crumbling. Termite- infested pews stood in uneven rows, decaying from lack of attention.

"Luke!" Grant called from across the nave.

Luke made his way amongst the maze of equipment and cords.

Grant waited just outside a wooden door. "Thought you'd like to see something we found."

"Lead the way," Luke said.

Grant opened the door into what Luke knew as the Sacristy or the priest's private office. A large desk sat in the middle of the room, a couch against the far wall, and a row of empty bookshelves. Grant waited for him to enter the room and looked to him.

"What?"

"Wait for it," Grant said, followed by an audible click like the release of a door. The bookcase swung outward, revealing a hidden passage.

"Seriously?"

"Oh, no, it gets better. Follow me," Grant said, flipping on his high-powered flashlight.

They followed the small hallway to another room. On the far wall, Luke saw a shadow. Before he had to say anything, Grant shone his light on the objects. It was two huge steel levers sitting side by side. One was pointing upward. The other pointed down.

"What is that?" Luke asked.

"Think about it," Grant challenged with a small grin.

Luke thought for a moment. "Have you tested it yet?"

"They won't move," Grant said. "I had Craig grease them up and everything. Will not budge."

Luke squatted next to the levers, taking a closer look. "If that's the case, how the hell were they activated when Claire stood over the well?"

"Good question," Grant said. "I think the one is for the top grate, and the second is for the other end of the chute.

"Someone would've had to move this lever to drop Claire into the well, then move it again to close the grate when the well filled with water."

"Then the second lever would be activated when the contents of the well emptied into the river below the falls," Grant added. "Besides the minor fact that the bookshelf hasn't moved in ages, there was no one here."

"You're sure?"

"Yeah, come here," Grant said, leading them back out the passage. "See the dust?"

Luke knelt, looking at the path created by the door's movement.

"This here was from the movement today when we found it. If it had moved sometime recently, the dust would not be nearly as thick. We would be able to see the line the door creates when it opens."

"I have to admit this is a new one," Luke admitted.

"This place is full of surprises," Grant said.

"Yeah? What else did you find?"

"There is a whole separate living area on the other side of this wall. Craig is working on it now. Did you check in on Claire?"

"Yeah, she's fine. The press is scheduled to leave within the hour. She called the vet, and Pip is doing good," Luke replied.

"Good," Grant said. "I'm thinking about the teams. Due to the nature of the situation, I think one member of the main team should be with each of the minor teams just in case something happens. I'm going to pair you with Kate and Evan if that's okay."

"Sounds good."

"Will and Ashley will be in the truck with Claire. Shaun will be with Glen and Maggie, and I will be with Amy and Brian. We have Craig, Alex, Serena, and Matt on Cameras and Justin, Greg, and Thor on booms."

"Thor?"

"Yep."

"Does he?"

"Oh, yeah, he embraces the look, great boom."

"As long as he is good at the job, right?"

"Exactly," Grant said with a grin.

Static came over the walkie-talkie, then Craig's voice.

"We just cracked the lock to the living quarters."

"Thanks, I'll be right there," Grant replied into the device. "You coming?"

"No, actually. I'm gonna hang out in here for a few minutes."

"Enjoy," Grant said before leaving the office.

On every investigation, big or small, Grant Henley's priority was always the safety of his team. Splitting the central team into mini-teams posed the best option. If anything happened on any of the walks, an experienced team member would be present to handle the situation. While he hand-picked and trusted every member of his team, he also knew in the face of pure evil or peril, people could freeze, loose reason, and panic. It was only human nature. He needed to anticipate all the possibilities.

He would not admit aloud to the team, but the investigation of Crestwater Church would most likely be one of the most intense and riskiest endeavors many of them would ever experience.

"What have we got?" Grant asked, entering the open door on the opposite side of the altar from where he'd just been with Luke.

"Dust, and lots of it," Craig replied, standing triumphant and placing the bolt cutters against the wall. *Finders'* investigators Brian, Glen, and Maggie were standing with him, having assisted in the excavation.

"Let's take a look," Grant said, turning on his flashlight again and leading the way into the area. He'd expected a wooden floor but found it to be solid rock. Good news meant they wouldn't have to worry about falling through any holes in an old weakening wooden floor.

They ventured inside, and the dust began to settle, revealing the scant contents of the room. Walking around, they found a few small single beds, broken empty dressers, and a cracked mirror on the far wall. Grant took a few steps toward the far wall and stopped. He raised his hand in a hold position, signaling for everyone to stop. Listening, he waited and heard it again, louder this time, definitely a growl. He swung the flashlight toward the sound and stopped, illuminating a snarling, growling dog. The light flashed red in its eyes. Grant stepped back. "Out, get out. Slowly and quietly leave the room," he said in a low tone to the rest of the group.

In his peripheral vision, he watched the group of three slowly back out of the room. Keeping eye contact with the still angry animal, he began with a first step back, simultaneously searching for anything he could put between himself and the animal.

The bed to his left was close enough he would be able to skirt it between them, giving him a few seconds to exit the space. Two more steps and he could reach the bed. He felt someone enter the room and saw Luke's outline slowly approaching him.

"The bed," Luke said, knowing his plan.

"Yes."

"Move fast."

"Not a problem," Grant replied.

The dog inched forward, getting ready to strike.

"On three," Luke said, and Grant silently nodded. He mapped out in his mind how this was going to work. "Ready?"

"Yeah, okay . . . one . . ."

"Two."

"Three."

Grant lunged for the bed, flipping it on its side and dashed. Without warning, something grabbed his ankle. He fell to his knees, giving the dog a chance to strike.

Luke watched the bed flip on its side, creating a temporary barrier. Luke, bolt cutters in hand, watched and waited. Grant fell to his knees. The dog caught Grant's ankle before Luke could bridge the gap. The dog's jaws were locked. Grant struggled to get out of the dog's grip. Luke stepped between the two and swung the cutter at the dog's head to get the hound to release. Luke hit the dog harder and harder, with no effect and no damage to the animal.

Luke stopped, holding his cross. "In the name of the Lord Jesus Christ of Nazareth, I stand with the power of the Lord God Almighty to bind Satan and all his evil spirits, demonic forces, satanic powers, principalities, along with all kings and princes of terrors, from the air, water, fire, ground, nether-world, and the evil forces of nature."

The dog continued to bite down, and Grant bellowed in pain. "Fuck!"

"I take authority over all demonic assignments and func-tions of destruction sent against me, and I expose all demonic forces as weakened, defeated enemies of Jesus Christ. I stand with the power of the Lord God Almighty to bind together all enemies of Christ present here, all demonic entities under their one and highest authority, and I command these spirits into the abyss to never again return."

The dog whined in pain, released Grant's leg, and scurried behind the bed. Luke grasped Grant's hand, pulling him to his feet and out the door. They slammed the door shut in unison. Something heavy and strong banged against it, push-ing to get out. "What do we do?" Craig asked.

"Find something to wedge against the door," Luke called. Glen and Brian helped to hold the door closed. The pounding continued. "Get the salt!"

Craig disappeared with Maggie out the door. Luke started a prayer to bless the door. The pushing and banging stopped just as Maggie and Craig reappeared. "Is it over?"

"Doesn't matter," Grant said, motioning to Craig for the piece of wood he'd brought to wedge the door closed. Grant took the piece and positioned the wood against the door to keep it closed. "Go get the nail gun out of the truck."

"You got it, Boss," Craig said with a nod.

"You have the salt?" Luke asked Maggie. She nodded, face pale. Giving the clear glass jar to him with shaking hands, he gave her a reassuring nod. "We've got this. Go take a break."

Luke opened the salt and poured it against the threshold.

"Not very Christian of you," Brian commented.

"Actually, for centuries since the advent of Jesus, salt that had been cleansed and sanctified by special exorcisms and prayers was given to catechumens before entering the church for baptism. According to the fifth canon of the Third Council of Carthage in the third century, salt was administered to the catechumens several times a year, a process attested by Augustine of Hippo."

Craig returned with the nail gun and handed it to Grant, who started nailing the door.

Luke continued, "Two specific rites, namely a cross traced on the forehead and a taste of blessed salt, not only marked the entrance into the catechumenate but were repeated regularly. By his own account, Augustine was "blessed regularly with the Sign of the Cross and seasoned with God's salt. Therefore, it is very Christian of me."

Grant finished securing his side of the door and handed Luke the nail gun.

"Early in the sixth century, John the Deacon also explained the use of blessed salt. he said *So the mind which is drenched and weakened by the waves of this world is held steady.*"

"That is blessed salt?"

"Yep, take it wherever I go," Luke replied.

"Consider me schooled," Brian said.

"What happened in there?" Glen asked.

"Stray dog," Craig quickly said from behind Glen. "It happens in these abandoned buildings. A dog or raccoon gets trapped inside and is relatively pissed off when someone finds it. Greg could use your help in the vestibule. We'll finish up here." Glen and Brian nodded and exited the room. "All secure?"

"Yep, let's get you outside to wrap up that ankle," Luke said, offering Grant his shoulder.

"Claire's gonna be pissed," Grant said.

Claire jumped out of the back of the van as they exited the church, running to them. Her heart had started pounding as soon as she saw Luke assisting Grant across the inside of the church on the monitors.

"What the hell happened?" Claire asked, taking Grant's other arm assisting in the hobbling to the van.

"Stray dog," Luke said, lying to Claire.

"What? Did it bite you?"

"Got me in the ankle," Grant said, easing onto the edge of the van's opening.

Claire hopped into the back of the van to grab the medkit. She returned as Luke removed Grant's shoe and sock before lifting his pant leg to reveal the extent of the damage.

"It doesn't look bad. Bleeding has already stopped," Luke said. "Some antiseptic and a few bandages, maybe a dinosaur bandage, and you will be good as new."

Grant chuckled at the comment.

"So not funny," Claire scolded. "How bad does it hurt? We need to have the dog tested for rabies and other diseases. I'm calling animal control." She watched the two men exchange glances and then stopped dialing her phone. "Wait, what are you not telling me?"

"Well, first, the dog is locked securely in the room where we found it," Grant said. "We nailed the door shut and wedged some wood against the door."

"Okay," Claire said, still confused and folding her arms against her chest. "Good. Kudos to you for securing the threat. What's the catch?"

"Odds are if animal control goes back into the room, there will be no dog."

"What? But you said . . ." Claire started, and the door of the church opened.

Shaun stepped out, joining the group. "You called?" he asked and then saw Grant's ankle. "Are you okay?"

"I'm good," Grant answered. "Luke, do you want to handle this?"

"Yeah, I got it," he said, looking to Claire before pulling Shaun aside.

"What the hell is going on?" Claire demanded.

"There was what appeared to be a dog in a room we were investigating," Grant started to explain. "Problem is, the room was sealed from the outside for a very long time."

"The dog was trapped in there when they sealed it up?"

"No, the room was sealed, as in no air has been in the room for over a decade and there was no way for the dog to get into the area from the outside. There were no holes or other entrances to the room. It was solid stone," Grant said.

"You are telling me it wasn't a dog that attacked you. It was something else."

"Still a working theory, but yes," Grant replied.

"What are Luke and Shaun doing?"

"Luke already sealed the room with a blessing and blessed salt. He is going to have Shaun examine the outer area and cleanse the space with sage. It should keep whatever contained."

"Should?" Claire questioned.

"Yes."

Claire turned in frustration, her anxiety about the situation steadily rising.

"What do you want me to say, Claire?"

"I have no idea what I want you to say," she said, turning to face him. "It's not even sundown. The electricity keeps going out. There are problems with all of the equipment. Now Demon dogs are attacking the team. I honestly have no idea of anything you could say to make any of this better, save let's pack up and get the hell out of here."

"You know we can't do that," Grant said. "There's too much at stake now. Too many lives have been affected by this thing. We have to try and end it."

Claire took a deep breath, weighing her next words. "Can we? Tell me the truth. Do you honestly think we can end it?"

"I truly do believe we can put an end to all of this. No one else will get hurt, nothing else will ever happen because of this damn menace. I believe we are this town's best chance." His voice was full of conviction and honesty, and she felt a little stronger.

"Okay, then we keep going, but if one more person gets attacked or injured, we pull the plug. Deal?"

"Deal."

"Let's get you fitted with that dinosaur band-aid and get back to work," Claire replied, opening the medkit.

An hour later, the media was gone, and they were ready for lights out. The sun was beginning to set, and Grant pulled the team into a circle in front of the church for a team huddle.

"As many of you know, there have been several circumstances and revelations leading us to this point. All of that aside, we've got a long night ahead of us. Crestwater Church, as you have all realized, is a monster of a building. Regardless of any circumstances surrounding this investigation, regardless of anything you've heard or even seen, this investigation goes by the book. Number one is safety first. No one is to be in the church at any time alone or isolated. You walk into a room together. You exit a room together. That includes camera and boom. I know you like to hang back for the shot. Not tonight. No wandering off, no exploring. Keep in constant contact. Westin Media has sprung for these high-tech communication devices used by the presidential secret service. The truck will be monitoring all of the activity. Something happens, you report in first and then investigate. Not the other way around. We have been lax in the protocol in the past. Not tonight. If there is a problem, report it immediately. If you lose comms, you have a backup walkie-talkie. Check-ins will be at ten-minute intervals, no exceptions."

Many of the members groaned.

"I know check-ins suck and interrupt the flow, but it takes two seconds. You can deal with it for one night. We have a team lead for each walk. Two of you will be with either myself, Shaun Levy, or Luke Melloy. Claire, Will, and Ashley will be in the truck. If any team lead or anyone from the truck announces a code red, you are to exit the building immediately. No questions. Exit as quickly as possible and regroup back here. Any questions?"

"Grant, we've all heard the rumors and know what they found. I mean, it's all over the media. What do you think is happening here?" Thor asked from the back of the group.

"You are my team, and we're alone. Here's the scoop, team. We believe we are dealing with an ancient, very powerful high-level Demon that has existed here for centuries. It is evil. This town, this populace, and a teenage girl need our help to expose and get rid of this thing. They are why we're here. What we signed up for. It's not about the cameras, social media feeds, or even the scare. *Finders* is about helping people, and that is what we are going to do. *Finders* has the best investigation team in the world. We have a trained physical medium and an experienced demonologist on hand. As long as we all follow the rules, we'll be fine. We will succeed. If there is anyone who would like to walk away from this investigation, there will be no judgments, no retribution, or hard feelings. Walk away now, or I'll assume you are aware of the risks and ready to fight the good fight."

The team remained silent.

After a moment, Grant stepped forward extending his hands. "Okay, let's have a team prayer. Luke, would you do the honors, please?"

Luke and every member of the team joined hands in unison and bowed their heads, "Our Father, please guide our steps, purify our intentions and protect every member of this team who fights against the evil that has dwelt in this place for too long. We walk and fight in your name. Dear Lord, give us the strength and protection to ensure our success and safe return from this journey. Amen."

"Amen," Grant said echoed by the rest of the group. They broke hands. "Lights out."

Claire, Ashley, and Will worked steadily with the monitoring. Each set of eyes had its own set of monitors to watch. Their jobs were to write the timestamp of anything they saw, heard, or noticed. If something was happening, they were to alert the team in the affected area to investigate.

They were on hour four of the investigation, and nothing was moving. The whole team took a break. Doubts about the threat of the church began to emerge from the groups. Luke, Grant, and Shaun remained silent. After everyone finished eating and talking, the teams were getting ready to reassemble. Luke, Shaun, and Grant walked toward Claire, who stood at the back of the truck.

"What are you thinking?" Claire asked, looking at the three men.

"Don't know. This stuff doesn't happen on cue. You know that. You've done enough of these with us to know sometimes it just doesn't happen the way we expect it to."

"It's hiding," Shaun said. "It's in there. It's waiting for something."

"Can you see it?" Claire asked.

"No, but I can feel it. It's like a distant constant hum," Shaun replied.

"It's getting them comfortable. The team's guards are down. It knows we're here, and it's patient."

"We stay vigilant and keep going," Grant said. "Let's get back in there."

The teams headed back inside.

Claire's team was Team Two, consisting of Shaun, Maggie, Glen, Thor on boom, and Alex on camera. Team One and Team Three entered the church independently, each having designated the back areas of the church. Team Two was the last to enter, having been slated with the main congregation area, the nave.

CHAPTER ELEVEN

Shaun Levy entered the nave with his team of four. Camera and boom always stayed behind them. He had a plan of attack, wanting first to investigate the infamous well. They moved to the right side of the nave toward the broken floor. They approached and slowed inspecting the area.

"This is it?" Maggie asked, stopping a few feet away in hesitation. A small thin girl with dark-rimmed glasses, jet black hair, and numerous tattoos, she was the millennial ghost hunter of the group. Curious, usually with nerves of steel, she seemed put off by the well.

"This is the well," Glen said. In his mid-twenties, tall and lanky, with dirty brown hair and a full beard to match, he walked up to the edge and squatted to inspect the grate atop the opening. Glen's signature move was to get the entities to materialize by verbally harassing them.

"Is it safe?" Maggie asked.

"Yeah, they came in and checked the area around the well for any other weak spots before we arrived. All good," Glen said, taking a seat on the edge of the well. "What's the word, Shaun?"

"It is the well where all of those people died. I'm getting cold blackness, shivering cold, pain, fear, and panic. Let's try an EVP session. Maggie, set up the K2 meter on the edge of the well, and let's see what happens." Maggie reluctantly did as asked but stepped quickly back once complete. "Glen, scan the area with the EMF. See if you get any abnormal readings but stay close."

"Ten-four, Chief," Glen replied, getting out his EMF detector.

"Maggie, do you want to lead the questioning?" Shaun asked. Maggie gulped and nodded. "Whenever you're ready."

He watched the girl compose herself, take a seat on the floor, and take a breath, "Is there anyone here who would like to talk to us?" They waited. "We are here to help you. If you are scared or trapped, we want to help you. We are not here to hurt you." They waited. "There is a toy on the edge of the well. If you can, try to make it light up to let us know you are here." They waited.

The K2 flashed.

"That's right! Can you do it again?" Maggie asked. Glen circled back around to them.

"You get anything?" Shaun asked.

"Nothing unusual," Glen said.

"Please try again, we want to talk to you," Maggie repeated, and Shaun motioned for Glen to take the infra-red camera from him. Glen took the camera. The lights of the K2 flashed again, stronger this time.

"Team Two checking in. Getting a response on the K2, over," Shaun said.

"Roger that, team lead. Okay to proceed with caution, over."

"Copy that, proceeding, over."

"Thank you. Can we ask you some questions?" Maggie said, and the K2 immediately flashed. "Are you one of the people who died here?"

The K2 meter flashed again.

"Were you murdered here by the priest who used to lead this church?"

The K2 flashed again.

"Are you trapped here?"

The K2 flashed again, brighter this time.

Shaun closed his eyes, wanting to connect with the spirit. The images were foggy and dark, but he could see a small golden-haired child standing atop the well. Red blood gushed from his throat. He was pointing in Shaun's direction. Within moments there were four or five, then ten, fifteen children standing on and around the well looking at him, pointing.

Shaun opened his eyes.

The K2 flew off the well and across the room. A loud, audible rumbling erupted around them, and before he could react, cold water spouted upward like a geyser from the well, knocking them all off their feet.

Grant entered with the rest of Team One. They crossed the nave and headed back to the Sacristy, where traditionally the church's relics were stored, along with robes and the clergy's private offices. He was anxious to get into the catacombs beneath the church.

Grant led the way through the main room and out a secondary door in the back of the Sacristy. They descended about two dozen concrete steps before entering an open area. He stopped and waited for the rest of the team. "The catacombs are made up of long, narrow winding halls opening into crypts like this one. We stay together. We take our time and keep our eyes and ears open. I'll take the lead with the camera. Amy, you use the recorder. Brian, you are in charge of the K2."

The team nodded and headed in, Grant leading the way. Grant had to walk sideways due to the narrowness of the hallway. They arrived at the first opening, finding several remains laid in separate shelves against the wall.

"Who are these people?" Amy asked.

"Catacombs were usually used for the burial of clergy and

the rich. It offered additional security versus an open and exposed grave. People would donate heavily to reside down here. They were also said to be used for the truly evil, thinking the sanctity of the church would trap them in the church and prevent them from haunting the living," Brian replied.

Grant focused on the camera but smiled inwardly, knowing Brian had done his homework. One of his first recruits over ten years ago, Brian was eager for knowledge and tried very hard to impress Grant every chance he got. Grant was happy for the enthusiasm and made sure to include him on as many investigations as he could. Brian also had a massive crush on Amy.

Amy was a determined, hard-working brunette with a great, helpful positive attitude. She was working on her thesis in paranormal psychology and was quickly becoming an expert in her field. Her membership on the team helped with the fame, but she was levelheaded enough to not give in to the hype. She was in it for the science.

An odd noise broke Grant's thought, and he shushed them both. They waited while the audible sound echoed off the walls. It was a wail. They all looked at each other. Grant led the way toward the sound. They moved quickly through the stone hall, the sharp rocks scraping and scratching against their arms. The closer they got, the further away the noise seemed to be. "Team Three checking in. Wailing noise in the catacombs. Over."

"Roger that, Team Three. Okay to investigate, over."

"Copy that. Starting investigation, over."

Grant stopped, examining the blackness ahead of them. He saw movement on the infra-red camera. A shadow peered from around the next corner. "Is someone down here?"

There was no response.

"Grant, look," Brian said, getting his attention. The K2 meter flashed repeatedly.

A full-fledged howling echoed off the walls, causing them all to cringe and cover their ears. It stopped. Grant looked to his team.

"It came from behind us," Craig said. Grant turned to see Craig's back turned to them.

He didn't like this. They were trapped in this little space, "Okay, everyone, follow me." He led them forward toward the area where he'd seen the shadow on his camera. They turned into the open space and faced each other.

"Whatever it was, it's gone," Brian said. "The K2 is dead."

"Switch to the EMF," Grant said. Looking at his camera, he saw the battery had gone from a 92% charge to a 60% charge within a few moments. "Okay, group decision time. Do you want to keep going or turn back?"

"Keep going, definitely," Amy said.

"Keep going," Brian agreed.

"You guys good?" Grant asked the camera and boom.

"We're golden," Craig replied for the pair.

"Okay, let's keep going," Grant said, leading the way once again out of the opening. Camera up, he looked for any signs of movement. After a few meters, a figure darted out of one of the openings and started running down the hall away from them. "Son of a bitch, someone is down here!"

Grant went charging after the culprit, the team in tow. He chased the figure for a good fifty yards when the ground rumbled beneath them. The entire group stopped.

"Earthquake?" Brian asked.

"In Wyoming?" Amy said.

Suddenly they heard a yelp of pain. They all turned to see Justin, the boom operator, face down on the ground. Craig moved to his side and yelped as something pulled him out of their vision and into the darkness. Amy screamed. Brian fell back against the wall.

"Craig!" Grant yelled. "Brian, grab Justin and head back to

the last opening. Amy, help him!"

"Team Three, Red Alert, Red Alert! Everyone out, over!" Grant called, turning on his flashlight in search of Craig. He followed Amy and Brian into the closest opening.

"He's unconscious but breathing," Amy said.

"What do we do?" Brian asked.

"We get out of here," Grant replied, assessing the situation. His ears alerted him to another sound. It took him a moment to realize what it was. Rushing water. Using his flashlight, he peered into the darkness, seeing a familiar figure standing a few feet away from him, smiling. She looked skeletal, broken, and bruised, like a living corpse — Kelsey James. She laughed aloud, the crackling sound filling up the enclosed space. Grant's blood went cold when the wall of water engulfed her and came rushing toward them. "Get against the wall and grab hold of something."

"What's happen —" Amy started, but was quickly silenced, the violent force of water engulfing the room.

Luke Melloy opened the door to the Sacristy, and lightning flashed just outside illuminating the large room.

"That's not ominous or anything," Kate said, entering the room just behind him, followed by Evan, Matt, and Greg.

"It's mood lighting," Evan said.

"Okay, Creeper," Kate said.

"Who wants this thing?" Luke asked, holding out the camera.

"I'll take it," Evan said. "What is this room, anyway?"

"This is the Sacristy, where all of the religious artifacts, robes, and documents were stored."

"Is this where he would've kept the log Claire found at the Library?" Kate asked.

"Probably," Luke replied.

"You called me a Creeper," Evan said.

Luke rolled his eyes a little, trying to concentrate. He knew they couldn't help it, and he couldn't blame them. At this point, this whole night was a collection of ghost stories, rumors, and conjecture. For him, this was a night of clues and strategy. He was still struggling to uncover the truth behind the Demon's motivations. He heard his mentor's voice in his head.

The demonic do not have a sense of reason. There is no logic to demonic motivations. They are predators and have one purpose, the destruction of God's Kingdom.

"Let's get settled in and start with an EVP session," Luke suggested.

The team did as directed, setting up the K2 on the desk and starting the recording. Kate and Evan took turns asking questions in an attempt to prompt a response.

Luke was half-listening deep in thought and analyzing all of the events leading up to this moment. Piece by piece, he saw the picture forming.

"I was just thinking about something Shaun said to me about being a living superhero."

"You are," Luke said.

"Yeah? In all of the superhero movies I've seen, the hero can destroy the villain not vanquish it to live another day," Claire said. *"But I'm quickly learning. Real life is nothing like the movies."*

His mind immediately focused on the first time he'd touched Claire, the surge of warmth and connection that had flowed through him. Then at the Taylor house, the rise of electricity that hit him when Claire took his hand against the Demon in the attic.

No.

Luke snapped out of his head, hearing a scream. Evan was on top of Kate, his hands in a stranglehold. Kate struggled against him to no avail. Both the cameraman and the boom operator were attempting to pull him off. Evan shoved them both away into the far corners of the room. Each man crumpled in a heap, unconscious.

"Evan, stop!" Luke said, grabbing his shoulders and pulling. "Evan, stop!"

Evan released his grip on Kate, throwing Luke off his back with unearthly strength. Luke stumbled, catching himself against the desk. Evan was not a small guy, but physically, Luke was superior. Evan heaved himself off the floor and turned to face Luke. His eyes black, he lunged for Luke, hitting him in the stomach with his shoulder. Luke didn't move. The desk did. Luke used the imbalance to roll to his right, straddling Evan to the ground. "Kate, run! Base Ops. Red Alert. Red Alert, everyone out, over!"

Luke attempted to hold Evan down but once again was thrown off, slamming into the fireplace. He heard Kate struggling with the door. The door would not budge. Evan stomped forward, lifting Luke off the ground by his neck. Luke struggled, kicking and clawing at the man. Finally getting some momentum, he lifted his legs and pushed the man off him. Gasping for air, he looked to the adjacent catacomb door, hoping Grant would arrive any moment to assist.

A loud rumbling shook the ground and walls around them. Kate screamed. The eruption didn't faze Evan. He walked to the nearest bookshelf and ripped a shelf off the brackets. Luke grabbed for his flashlight.

"In the name of God, in the name of Jesus Christ, I cast you out, Demon! Release this innocent from your hold! I cast you back to Hell! In the name of all that is holy and right, I cast you out!"

The rumbling stopped. Evan collapsed to the floor. Luke's head fell back to the floor. His entire body hurt, but he was vaguely aware. He heard sniffling, and saw Kate curled against the door, crying.

Shit.

Luke lifted himself off the floor. Moving to Kate, he put an arm around her in reassurance. "Team One checking in. Is anyone out there? Over. Claire, Will, Grant, Shaun can anyone hear me? Over." A crackling followed by loud feedback caused him to yank the earpiece out of his ear. He felt Kate stiffen beside him and looked up.

Kelsey James stood in the middle of the room, silently staring, looking grotesque as if someone had turned her inside out, putting her skin on the wrong way. Luke silently echoed Kate's alarm. He stood, shielding Kate behind him.

"Kelsey, what are you doing here?"

"Hello, Luke," she said, her voice deep and crackling. "Let the games begin."

CHAPTER TWELVE

Claire stared at the monitors. She felt a headache coming on and reached for some pain medicine in her bag.

Rummaging around, she touched something she didn't recognize and pulled it from her bag. A flash of images swam across her mind.

Kelsey James standing at the altar inside the church, a dagger in hand she chanted and cut, then squeezed her hand, the blood gushing over her palm onto the altar. A Demon rose from the darkness. Towering, black and snarling, he smiled at her. Kelsey stepped back. Her eyes watered in realization as to what she'd conjured. Her fear paralyzed her. She couldn't move as the Demon approached and lifted her off the ground like a ragdoll. Claire found herself inside Kelsey's body. Her flesh turned to fire. Her heart pounded as he manifested himself inside her body. The pain was agony, blinding, all-consuming. Then there was blackness.

In the blackness, she heard its voice. "You will lure them here. Make them come. You will be truth's end, my sweet."

Claire jerked and dropped the item on the floor. Her eyes opened. She saw the candle she'd stolen from Kelsey James' room. Claire looked around and found herself alone in the van. "Will? Ashley?" Feeling like an idiot looking for the pair in the small space, she knew they were gone.

No matter what happens, what you hear or see you are not to leave the van or come inside the church.

She gulped back her fear—she'd never thought of a

situation where she would question Luke's request. Where had they gone?

Monitors. Check the monitors. Cameras and media equipment surround us.

The monitors were fuzz, static, offline.

Claire immediately tried comms. No answer. The walkie-talkie — nothing.

Silence.

Dread crawled up her spine. She debated her options. She couldn't just sit there and wait.

No matter what happens, what you hear or see, you are not to leave the van or come inside the church.

Luke's words echoed in her mind, followed by the words of the Demon.

You will lure them here. Make them come. You will be truth's end, my sweet.

Fuck it

Claire grabbed a flashlight and an extra pack of equipment before pushing open the door. Stepping out of the van and onto the ground, she turned on the flashlight and saw the glistening of white on the ground. It circled the van. She'd stepped across the line of salt.

Oh, God.

A blast of pain hit her face from the right, knocking her back against the van. She stumbled and rolled onto the ground seeing stars.

"I knew I could get you to come out," Kelsey James said, standing over her staring. "You stupid bitch."

Claire kicked Kelsey in the shin and heard a crack. Kelsey staggered back before running into the church. Claire grabbed the flashlight and went after her. Cautiously opening the door, she stepped inside. Immediately recognizing her surrounding from her excursion with Pip, she saw the main vestibule doors closed. Checking the area around her, she saw nothing. Moving to the doors, she pulled on the large brass handle. They moved with ease, as if inviting her into the house of God. Her heart racing, she heard her name echoed off the walls of the expanse.

"Come out, Kelsey. I'm not in the mood for games. Come out and let's finish this. I know what happened. It was an accident. You didn't mean for this to happen. You can still fight him — it. You're still alive in there. I believe in your strength, Kelsey. You can come back from this." Claire said and heard a crackling laugh.

"Claire."

Using the flashlight to scan the room, she saw nothing. It was empty.

"Over here, Claire," something whispered in her ear, sending another chill up her spine and causing her to turn to the left and point the light at space.

"Fight it, Kelsey. We can both get out of this, but you have to fight it," Claire said, still searching. Turning to the right, she heard something. "Kelsey?"

"Nope," she heard from above her. Shining her light above, she saw the Demon from her vision, hanging from the rafter above her head. It dropped down, taking her down with it.

When Claire opened her eyes again, she stared into the blackness. Her head throbbed, and she was wet and cold. Struggling to sit up, she looked around, searching for a source of light. Lightning flashed through the oversized windows. Shaun was beside her, unconscious on the ground.

"Oh, my God, Shaun!" Moving to him, she immediately checked his pulse. It was there, steady and strong. Shaun's hand shot up from the floor, wrapping around Claire's neck. Her air supply gone, she could feel the bones in her neck strain in his strong grip. Claire struggled to remove his hand when his eyes opened. She didn't see the warmth of brown she remembered, only blackness.

"Hello, Claire. Gawd, you are a weakling. Two hits were all it took to knock you out cold. I've been waiting forever for you to wake up!" he said, his voice dark and garbled.

Lifting her above him, he tossed her aside. She hit the floor hard, knocking the air from her lungs.

"I couldn't wait to show you what I've done with the place. Decorating is not my forte, but I couldn't resist making this as amazingly painful for you as possible." He picked up the flashlight from the ground and turned it on. "First, we have sarcastic Glen. He spewed all kinds of obscenities when I strung him up."

The Demon inside Shaun shined the light into the far left corner of the church where Glen hung. He was nailed to the side of the church wall, one nail in each wrist, and one in his overlapped feet. Tears of agony streamed down her face with all of her nightmares manifesting before her eyes.

"Next, we have enlightened Maggie. She is a screamer. Yes, she is. I have to admit I'd like to see her in the throes of passion, but only time will tell if she will completely capture my heart as you have, dearest Claire," the Demon said, shining the light behind him to the far right corner of the room where Maggie hung, also crucified against the wall, her throat slit, wet blood blanketing her chest.

"Over there in the back is Alex, poor sniffling Alex. He begged and begged to be spared. Even tried to make a deal with the devil, literally, but I don't do deals. It is so hard these days to get people to pay up. There are all of these loopholes and double talk, really hasn't been worth the effort ever since Emperor Claudius. Negotiations have been a complete nightmare."

The Demon turned the light on the body that would be Alex. The corpse was missing its head. Claire's body heaved in revulsion.

"Don't like that one, huh? I may need to reconsider. Not sure where his head landed. I kinda just ripped and tossed, ya know?"

"Stop, please stop!"

"Last, but certainly not least. Especially with the name Thor! I have to say he did live up to his name. He fought hard, honorably, and took his death like a champ. His bowels will never be the same, but hey, he won't need them anymore. Right? No harm? No foul." Shaun squatted down next to her, like a coach counseling a student. "What do you think? I mean as far as artistic sense, I got it right on the money. I'm pleased with the overall effect and mood of the room. Anyway, I bet you are wondering where the rest of your merry men are hiding? They're scattered around the church in pieces. I was sure to leave enough for the authorities to give them a proper burial."

Claire had enough. The fear and anguish quickly turned to anger. "What is it you want? Why the spectacle? Surely you have better things to do with your infinite time in Hell!"

"Touché, my dear, I have always liked my women feisty."

"I am not, nor will I ever be your woman. Alive or dead. If you want me, why don't you kill me and get it over with?"

"Oh, that's right, I keep forgetting you don't know about the rules. Do you?"

"From my understanding, there are no rules. You can do whatever you want."

"You would think that, but there are those who are, let's say, protected."

"I am one of those protected? By whom?"

"The powers that be, God, Christ, Buddha, Allah, whatever it is you want to call it," the Demon replied. "You are special, Claire. Have you not figured this out yet? Girlfriend, how many more Mack trucks have to hit your dog?"

"Shut up! I'm not special. You're just weak!"

"I am infinite!"

"You are a lackey, an underling, a mindless slave to a soul-less, banished Master. You're evil and hateful because you were shunned and shut out, banished from the only heaven you will ever know. You knew love and devotion once, and now you live in a dark hole under the house of the power that banished you. I have He who banished you on my side. I have His strength, His power, and His love. You are the weak one, Demon, and I am the strong. In the name of all that is good, holy, loving, and powerful. I banish you back to Hell." Claire said, and the Demon bent in laughter.

"Do you think those words have any effect on me, little Clarinet? You are the medium, not the Demonologist, remember?"

"What did you say?"

"I said fuck you, Claire, and trust me, I will. Long and hard, until you scream for death!"

The welling fury in her gut burnt bright and hot. Her body vibrated in strength and electricity. She saw Shaun's eyes go wide. "I banish Thee in the name of the Father, the Son, and the Holy Spirit. I banish Thee spirit to leave the body of this innocent and return to your darkness!"

The Demon smiled, and then Claire watched Shaun's neck turn and snap.

"No!" Claire screamed, watching her friend and teacher fall to the ground. Her emotions unleashed in a blanket of pure light. The force threw her head back, extinguishing the darkness and bathing the world in fire.

Grant's eyes opened, and he coughed up water. Rolling to his side, he struggled to focus, remembering what had happened. A bright flashlight dimly illuminated the room around him, and he grabbed for it. He heard coughing to his right and left.

Flashing the light toward the sounds, he saw his team coming back to life. Amy, Brian, and even Justin were coming out of the blackness that had hit them so hard. "Is everyone okay?"

The trio replied between coughing fits and rose to their feet.

"What happened?" Justin asked, leaning heavily against the wall.

"It doesn't matter now. We need to find Craig and get out of here. Can you walk?"

"Yeah, I'm good," Justin replied, while Amy and Brian nodded.

"Let's go." Grant tugged the earpiece out of his ear and turned on the walkie-talkie. "Team Three checking in, copy? Team three calling base camp. Do you copy?" He got nothing but static. His heart raced and he quickened his steps. He knew what happened to them. He couldn't imagine what happened to the others. "Keep trying the walkies, all of you!"

They raced through the narrow halls and heard moaning. Grant moved faster, checking in each opening they passed.

"Come on, Craig, where are you, man?" Grant murmured to himself. They reached one of the openings, and the moaning increased. His light shone around the corner on a crumpled body in a heap on the floor. "Craig!"

Amy and Brian immediately went to the man's side.

"He seems groggy but okay," Amy said.

"Can you carry him out?"

"Definitely," Brian replied, and he and Amy lifted Craig against their shoulders, balancing him between them.

"You two good?" Grant asked.

"Let's go," Brian said.

Grant continued in a rushed fury toward the exit. He heard his name. He recognized the voice. "Grant, are you guys okay?"

"We're on our way to you!" Grant called back to Luke.

"Hurry!" Luke called.

They made it to the bottom of the steps in record time. Adrenaline notwithstanding, fear of another catastrophe was a definite motivator. Grant was the last to enter the room. He found Team One looking a little worse for wear than themselves.

"We need to get out of here," Grant said.

"We can't—the door is stuck," Kate announced.

"Everyone injured, move to the back of the room. Brian, Amy, Kate, and Luke, grab the corners of the desk," Grant ordered.

"What are we going to do?" Kate asked.

"We're gonna use the desk to break down the door," Brian replied.

"We need to flip it on its side and then lift. Got it?" Grant said, and everyone nodded. "Ready? On three. One, Two, Three." The team of five struggled to lift the ancient relic but finally got the momentum needed to flip it over. It landed hard on the floor.

"Fuck, that thing is heavy."

"Yeah, it is. That's good," Grant said.

"And bad," Luke said.

"Okay, we are gonna need everyone's help to do this. That door opens from the inside. The amount of force it's going to take to break through it is immense. It's going to take more than a few hits probably. I don't know what has or is happening out there. As soon as that door goes down, you run for the nearest door and get the hell out."

"What about you? You are coming with us, right?" Kate asked.

"Don't worry about us. Get the hell out of here. Do not, for any reason, come back in. Agreed?" Grant asked.

The group nodded. Grant and Luke locked gazes, not knowing what was going to happen next.

Claire opened her eyes, once again to blackness. As she turned her head and blinked away the fuzziness from her eyes, everything that had happened just moments before hit her like a mallet to the chest. Shaun's lifeless eyes stared back at her, and overwhelming grief and pain coursed through every vein in her body. She needed to move. She wanted to move, but the agony seemed to melt her into the cold stone beneath her body.

A whisper of cold air touched her cheek. Claire opened her eyes to see Kelsey straddling her, dagger in hand. Claire's hands instinctively shot up to defend against the impending blow. The dagger's blade sliced her arms repeatedly as she fought off the blows. She missed one of the strikes, and it pierced her shoulder. She screamed in agony before grabbing for the dagger. Catching hold of it, she also grabbed Kelsey's gripped hand in the process. Throwing her weight to the side, she pulled Kelsey over with her. Claire used her legs to push Kelsey away from her. The dagger pulled out of Claire's shoulder with a painful sucking noise. The knife fell between them.

A *bang* reverberating throughout the building took Kelsey's attention, and Claire grabbed the dagger from the floor. Lunging at Kelsey, Claire tackled her to the ground, hearing another loud *thud*. Kelsey grabbed at Claire's wrist, her hands turning to fire, scorching her wrists. Claire dropped the dagger, which clanked on the floor before she fell back, rolling out of the way.

With a third and fourth loud *thud*, she heard a *crash* and then saw feet running past where she lay on the ground.

"Claire!"

Within seconds she was lifted into Luke's strong arms. They were running for the doors just as they slammed shut.

Claire snapped out of her hazy state, jolting out of Luke's arms.

"Kelsey!"

He let her down, and Grant appeared next to them. She stood between the two men searching the church. "She's here. Careful, she—it likes to climb the walls." Claire said, using her light to illuminate the ceiling.

The trio stood back to back covering each other and watching for the next assault.

"What just happened?" Kate asked as they stepped into the thundering rain outside the church.

"Where are they?" Amy asked.

"We need to get help, now," Craig said, running to the media van. Throwing open the doors, he found an unconscious Ashley and Will inside. Amy and Brian went to the two team members while Craig fooled with the equipment. "Get the cell phones!"

"They won't work up here!" Kate said.

"911 will," Brian said.

"Find your cell phone and call 911. One of the carriers has got to get through," Craig said.

"What happened?" Will asked.

"Will, buddy we need your brain. We need to get the cameras working again," Craig said.

"What?" Will asked, his face scrunched in confusion.

"There is no time to explain. We need to see inside the church, now!" Amy said.

"Especially the nave!" Evan called.

Luke's flashlight swung upward a moment too late. Kelsey James was lying in wait. She leaped onto Grant's back. He struggled to get her off. Claire used her flashlight to hit the girl on the back of the head. Luke did the same. After a moment she fell and scurried away.

"Now what?" Grant said.

"I'm getting sick of this game," Luke said.

"Join the club," Claire said.

"We go on offense. Follow me."

Luke led the pair back to the sanctuary and the altar.

"This is where it happened," Claire said, touching the wax-stained altar.

"What happened?" Grant asked.

"I had a vision in the van. Kelsey was here. There were candles. She made an offering of blood. The Demon appeared. It wasn't her intent, but it was too late. It took over her body. That's what happened."

"Good to know," Grant said.

"There's something else," Claire began, and they heard a low resounding laugh.

Kelsey walked from the shadows and faced them. "Don't let me interrupt," Kelsey said in her normal teen voice. "Please continue with the story. I'm all ears."

"The Demon said *You will lure them here, make them come. You will be truth's end, my sweet.* It was all a trap. Everything, from the beginning, it was all a trap to get us here," Claire said, her back straightening in defiance.

"A trap for whom?"

"Us," Luke said. "Claire and I have something the Demon wants."

"I want nothing of you but your soul, human," Kelsey said, her demonic voice returning.

"That's a lie," Luke said, reaching for Claire's hand. Her body flew back without warning, hitting the marble wall behind them.

"All right, teenage Demon or not, I've had enough of this,"

Grant said, stepping forward at the Demon. He attacked, and the Demon defended. Luke took the distraction to go to Claire's aid. She sat against the marble wall, eyes closed.

"Claire, can you hear me?" he said, taking her face in his hands.

Her eyes opened.

"We need to finish this."

"Are you ready to kick some ass, Melloy?"

"Yes, oh, hell, yes," he said with a grin, helping her to her feet.

Grant sparred with Kelsey, matching her blow for blow. Grant hit hard. The sound of Kelsey's fragile bones cracking made him wince.

Watching, Claire asked, "How does this work?"

"I have no clue," Luke replied, taking her hand.

"Do what you know," Claire said.

"*Oratio ad Sanctum Michaelem Archangelum. In nomine Patris, et Filii, et in Spiritu sancto. Amen.,*" Luke recited the sacred words of the rite of exorcism. He feared Claire would get lost in words, but they seemed to fall off her lips as if she'd known them her whole life.

"*Princeps gloriosissime caelestis exercitus, Sancte Michael Archangele, da nobis aciem adversus principes potestates principes autem adversus mundi rectores tenebrarum harum, contra spiritualia nequitiae, in caelestibus,*" Luke and Claire continued in unison.

The energy building between them grew with every unified breath they took. "*Veni in auxilium hominum, quos Deus creavit ad eius est Instar et magnus apud quos redemit de tyrannide pretiumm diaboli. Te martyrum candidatus laudat exercitus sui custos, et quod ecclesia Sancti protector; tibi tradidit Dominus animas redemptorum in redemptionis Dominus duci in coelum.*"

Grant continued his attack on the Demon, pounding relentlessly and being equally pummeled.

"*Deus pacis conterat Satanam sub rogate ergo pedibus, captivos tenere homines non ut facias Ecclesia. Offer nostras preces in conspectu Altissimi, ut sine misericordia sumant super nos Apprehendam draconem serpentem antiquum qui est Diabolus et satanas, et ligátum mittas in abyssum proiecit Ut nemo se seducat amplius gentes. Sed exorcismus!"*

Luke's and Claire's words had a visible effect. The Demon thrashed uncontrollably, and its growls echoed off the walls of the church. Pain incited fury, and the Demon lashed out at full strength against Grant. In a few swift moves, the Demon dislocated Grant's arm, lifting him off the ground by his neck. Grant struggled and kicked, quickly losing air. Luke and Claire disconnected hands, rushing to assist him.

The Demon dropped Grant to the ground, turning its focus on Luke. The Demon raised his hand, palm outward. Luke grabbed at his chest, his face straining in pain. Lifted off the ground by an invisible force, his limbs extended and stretched outward. Luke screamed aloud as they audibly heard the bone ripping from the muscles of his arms.

Claire watched in horror before hurling herself at the Demon in an attempt to thwart the attack. The beast saw her coming and growled in laughter, swiping his fingers in the air. Claw marks appeared on Claire's neck and face. She fell to her knees. The Demon pushed his free hand outward, launching her off her place on the floor. She crashed into the altar with such force it cracked, collapsing on top of her as she hit the ground.

A melody of voices said in unison, "In the Name of Jesus Christ, our God and Lord, strengthened by the intercession of the Immaculate Virgin Mary, Mother of God, of Blessed Michael the Archangel, of the Blessed Apostles Peter and Paul and all the Saints. and powerful in the holy authority of our ministry, we confidently undertake to repulse the attacks and deceits of the devil."

The words hit the Demon hard enough for him to release his hold on Luke, sending him crashing to the ground.

The entire *Finders* team stood in the nave of the church, hands together, reciting the rite of exorcism. "Prayer to St. Michael the archangel. In the name of the Father, the Son, and the Holy Spirit. Amen. Prince of the heavenly host, Saint Michael the Archangel, give us the strength to battle against the power of the rulers of this world of darkness, against spiritual wickedness in high places."

Luke willed his body to move, watching the scene unfold. He spoke the recitation in Latin from the beginning, searching for Claire, and the team continued.

"I came to help men, whom God has made great progress, and it is among those freed from the tyranny pretium devil. The noble army of martyrs of her guardian and protector of the assembly, I entrusted the souls of the redemption to be led into the sky," the team continued.

Grant push his body off the floor, standing tall against the demonic force, reciting with them.

"So, I ask the God of peace to crush Satan under thy feet. Offer our prayers to the Most High, that without compassion upon us to take hold of the dragon, that ancient serpent, who is the devil and Satan. Chains into hurled themselves may no longer lead the people. Exorcism!"

They started the rite from the beginning again. On the second verse, Kelsey's body arched. Seeing the break in the Demon's strength, Luke pushed off the floor, searching for Claire. He found her amongst the rubble, covered in blood, her body bruised and covered in slashes.

"No, no, no." Luke fell to his knees, cradling her against him. He continued reciting the rite in Latin, mentally pushing his energy to her, sending her all the hope and love he carried for her tender soul. Claire stirred in his embrace. Her eyes opened. She said the words with him, as if they were speaking as one person.

Kelsey's arms lashed out, and an invisible dagger slashed

at Grant and the team. They staggered but did not cease.

Claire got to her feet, leaning on Luke. "That's it, Kelsey, fight him! We're here with you! You can win. You have to fight!"

Luke continued the prayer. They steadily walked toward the Demon. The Demon fought Kelsey for control, twisting and contorting her body.

"I promised you we'd get through this together. We're all here for you. Fight it, fight your way back to your life. Take back your soul, Kelsey," Claire said. "You are winning Kelsey, fight! You're almost home."

The Demon and Kelsey seemed to separate from each other, the one becoming two as Kelsey's body expelled the Demon from her soul.

"You're doing it, Kelsey, keep fighting! We're right here. Come back!" Claire shouted.

They came to the last verse, and Claire rejoined the prayer. The full force of the love in the church engulfed the Demon in white flames. Kelsey collapsed, and Grant rushed to catch her from hitting the floor. The entire team continued. The church beneath them rumbled and shook, the power of light and dark coming to a head.

"So, I ask the God of peace to crush Satan under thy feet. Offer our prayers to the Most High, that without compassion upon us to take hold of the dragon, that ancient serpent, who is the devil and Satan. Chains into hurled themselves may no longer lead the people. Exorcism!"

The Demon screamed and howled in agony.

"From the snares of the devil," Luke said alone. He and Claire stepped closer to the Demon.

"Deliver us, O Lord," the *Finders* Team replied.

"That Thy Church may serve Thee in peace and liberty," Luke said, his voice filling the area like thunder, with him and Claire only inches away from the writhing beast.

"We beseech Thee to hear us." The *Finders* Team replied.

"That Thou may crush down all enemies of Thy Church," Luke said. Claire's hand in his, they stood tall, a unified force against the entity.

"We beseech Thee to hear us," the *Finders* Team replied.

"Amen." The entire group finished. Claire and Luke reached out their free hands, touching the Demon at the same moment. The flames engulfing the corporal Demon exploded into a burst of white light, throwing Claire and Luke off their feet. The blinding light dissipated and then vanished.

Moments later the vestibule doors opened, and the church flooded with first responders and police.

CHAPTER THIRTEEN

In Shaun Levy's hometown in Illinois, the mourners stood around his rose covered mahogany casket in sorrow.

People of all walks of life came to pay their respects. The entire *Finders* team attended his funeral, as well as the services for their lost team members. Glen, Maggie, Alex, and Thor had been laid to rest the week before, a devastating blow in the wake of triumph.

The media was in full force at the funerals. The evidence tapes of what had happened at Crestwater Church that night were only known to the *Finders* team and the Crestwater Sheriff's Department. The footage would stay hidden under lock and key in Grant Henley's vault. The Crestwater Sheriff and *Finders* decided the world was not ready for what happened that evening, and the case concerning Kelsey James was closed. She was still recovering in the hospital from her injuries but would not suffer any lasting physical effects from her experience. Emotionally, it would be a hard road, but she had survived.

Grant took the pulpit. "In the words of George S. Patton, *it is foolish and wrong to mourn the men who died. Rather we should thank God that such men lived.* Shaun's life was blessed with the love of a family, friends, and life. A force greater than Shaun chose him to fight a battle many of us will never endure. He was constant, assured, and always loving. Knowing Shaun, he's looking down at everyone here today commenting on what we are all wearing or critiquing the flower arrangements. Shaun, we did our best for you, as you have always done for us. Once again, we will fall short to your brilliance. I hope you can forgive us and bless us with the wisdom of your life. You are loved and will be greatly missed by all the lives you touched so deeply. Farewell, my friend. Save some of the whiskey for when we join you."

Luke and Claire lay in each other's arms back at the hotel.

"I love you," Claire said.

"What?"

Claire adjusted her position to face him, "I said, I am in love with you, Luke Melloy. Is that a problem?"

"No, of course not," Luke said, pulling her close against him in a deep kiss. "I love you, too."

They drifted off together, exhaustion quickly taking hold.

The stench of death curled beneath his nose. Death would have to wait. Something told him twelve-year-old Jenny Ann Waster wasn't ready to die. She still had a full life ahead, despite this particular Demon's insistence she was already gone from this world and trapped in Hell.

Jenny Ann's skeletal form lurched from the padded bed in an attempted violent attack against her intended saviors.

"Luke, help me hold her down," the exorcist, Father Daniel, called to him. Luke immediately followed the priest's instruction, holding his arms against Jenny Ann's arms and chest, gently pushing the small girl back into the mattress. Jenny Ann seeming to relax. Father Daniel started reciting the prayer over the child. Inciting the Demon's wrath, the girl once against surged against Luke's hold. Luke repeated the prayer of the priest. The girl twisted and fought against him, releasing a deafening high-pitched scream that seemed to suck up all of the air in the room. The noise created agony. The two men instinctively covered their ears. The room erupted into chaos, the air around them turning violent, whipping at the men. Jenny Ann's attention directed to Luke. A low male voice echoed in

the room.

"He shall come and mark her with the sight of Heaven and Hell. His flesh to her flesh, she will be enslaved to only him upon the will of the father of darkened light."

The child wailed again bringing tears of pain to the men who crumpled, paralyzed.

"She will be water and air. You will suffocate and shrivel, drown and fall from your grace in her name. The darkness will claim your soul."

Another unearthly scream raked their senses as if the child were calling out to death himself. A final breath, and the chaos stopped.

Luke's eyes opened in the darkness. His heart pounding from the reoccurring dream, he struggled to calm his breathing. Claire's warm body snuggled against him, and he moved carefully not to wake her. Rolling out of bed, he walked into the bathroom and flicked on the light. Turning on the faucet, he splashed water on his face and, staring at his reflection, he questioned his whole life.

I love you, Luke Melloy

The words brought such pure joy to his heart and soul it was indescribable. Could it last?

Seeing movement in the reflection of the mirror, he watched Claire sit up on the side of the bed, her back turned to him.

Crap, I woke her

Exiting the bathroom, he clicked off the light and moved back toward the bed. "Hey sweetheart, I'm sorry if I woke you," he said. Claire stood from the bed and walked around the edge of the bed toward him. "Claire?"

"Hello, Daddy," she said, her voice a sweet growl, her eyes black and lifeless. "Did you miss me?"

"Jenny Ann?"

"You promised me you'd save me."

"No . . . this isn't . . ."

"You promised me!"

"Leave her alone!"

"She isn't yours! Is it her or me, Daddy? Who will you save now?"

To Be Continued . . .

ABOUT THE AUTHOR

Amy Romine has always wanted to be one of the good guys. From playing Charlie's Angels in the backyard of her Macungie, PA home as a child to the pages of her unending projects, Amy has always dreamed of adventure and romance. Her need to make the characters truly deserve their happiness takes us on many a twisted journey. From serial killers to demons, Amy holds nothing back in the name of true enduring love.

A mother of three, Amy has spent the past seventeen years working in Operations for Ricoh America's Corporation. She is an avid movie fan and enjoys books, television, theater, her dog, Pip, and all things romance.

https://amyjromine.blogspot.com/

Amy's Books

Trust Me Series:
Serenity Lost
Veiled Deception
Jaded Promises

Dead Air Collection
Shockwave
Backlash
Fallout

Soulmate Chronicles
Ever the Same
Come Undone

You Never Could Be (Stand Alone)
Little Angles (Stand Alone)

Coming Soon!

The Prophet and the Snow Angel
Gemini
The Cabin
Finders 2 — Return to Crestwater